SADIE X

Sadie X

Clara Dupuis-Morency
Translated by Aimee Wall

Literature in Translation Series

Book*hug Press

TORONTO 2023

First English Edition

Originally published as *Sadie X* © 2021 by Héliotrope
English translation © 2023 by Aimee Wall

This edition is published by arrangement with Héliotrope in conjunction with its duly
appointed agent Books And More Agency #BAM, Paris, France.

Library and Archives Canada Cataloguing in Publication

Title: Sadie X : a novel / Clara Dupuis-Morency ; translated by Aimee Wall.
Other titles: Sadie X. English
Names: Dupuis-Morency, Clara, 1986– author. | Wall, Aimee, translator.
Description: Translation of: Sadie X.
Identifiers: Canadiana (print) 2023022184X | Canadiana (ebook) 20230221858
    ISBN 9781771668477 (softcover)
    ISBN 9781771668484 (EPUB)
    ISBN 9781771668491 (PDF)
Classification: LCC PS8607.D9444 S3313 2023 | DDC C843/.6—dc23

The production of this book was made possible through the generous assistance of the Canada
Council for the Arts and the Ontario Arts Council. Book*hug Press also acknowledges the
support of the Government of Canada through the Canada Book Fund and the Government
of Ontario through the Ontario Book Publishing Tax Credit and the Ontario Book Fund.

Book*hug Press acknowledges that the land on which it operates is the traditional territory of
many nations, including the Mississaugas of the Credit, the Anishnabeg, the Chippewa, the
Haudenosaunee, and the Wendat peoples. We also recognize the enduring presence of many
diverse First Nations, Inuit, and Métis peoples, and are grateful for the opportunity to meet
and work on this territory.

To those in whom I live,
so that something else may exist.

NOTE

In 2013, scientists from the Genomics and Structural Information Laboratory at the Université Aix-Marseille discovered one of the largest viruses ever identified, a giant virus that is not only not pathogenic to humans but also does not care about us at all. They called it the Pandoravirus.

The name (chosen because this virus would "break the foundations of what we thought viruses were"), that is, the attempt to assign a definition to the discovery of a completely new reality, one that defies our previously held assumptions, and for which science does not yet have adequate language, makes this already the stuff of literature, a moment at which thought takes centre stage.

This novel borrows language from the brilliant work of these researchers, language that makes it possible to conceive of the Pandoravirus, to allow for its existence in our world.

Details of the characters' lives come from other stories, other situations.

PART 1

PANDORA

X X

Sadie is not a philosopher. Back when she was still studying philosophy, when she still thought it was her calling, one of her professors spoke about what he called the three humiliations of humanity. The first by Nicolaus Copernicus, who dethroned the Earth from its place at the centre of the universe, showing it was nothing more than a *tiny speck in a world-system*. The second by Charles Darwin, who spoke of our animal ancestor, destroying humanity's claim to a separate and superior status in creation. And the third by Sigmund Freud, who demoted the human "I" from its position as *master in its own home,* reducing it to dependency on *the most scanty information concerning all that goes on unconsciously in its psychic life.*

With this, Sadie's professor, an eccentric, broke down the walls of the discipline. It was rather unorthodox to venture into such scientific terrain within the Faculty of Philosophy. He emphasized the importance of each of these knowledge revolutions, fomented by the controversial work of each of these men and the resistance they faced. He repeated the word several times, hu-mil-i-A-tion, stressing the fourth syllable, building excitement until they could behold all of History stretching out before them, the chain formed by these summits, and identify the extraordinary moments in which thought had brought about radical change, these moments he called invidious, stubborn, ungrateful to the past, moments that, through the cataclysm created by this new vision, gave shape to the future.

After that slightly unusual course, Sadie never again heard anyone speak of the scientific revolution in the philosophy department, and she never again heard talk of science until the day she met François Régnier a few years later. She'd signed up for a seminar outside of her own program. Régnier was a physician working on research in France. During his semester on a fellowship at the Université francophone de la Montagne, he was appointed head of his first laboratory in Marseille. Régnier studied viruses.

X

He began the first class by presenting, without any preamble, an inventory of everything viruses lack and everything that there-fore disqualifies them from the category of living thing. His voice sounded rusty, as if he didn't use it often, his hands lifted from the table in jagged gestures, Sadie remembers it perfectly. A virus cannot be divided. A virus has no ribosomes, the little machines that read genetic code. A virus cannot translate its own code into activity. A virus does not reproduce by itself. A virus is not a cell. Régnier's nervous tics sent waves of unease through the classroom. Then, his litany of negations created a cadence. He persisted, holding that dissonant note. Régnier was not a handsome or particularly elegant man, but he had a distinctly erratic way of projecting himself into space, and the inventory of missing qualities he recited in a jittery, syncopated rhythm unsettled something in the composition of the air. There was an electricity in his words that disrupted the consistency of the present.

From one class to the next, Régnier's negative taxonomy became a poetic scansion that subtracted more and more with each utterance. He excluded more and more qualities of the living from the virus, creating for the students a continually diminishing figure. They began to expect that by the end of the semester they would arrive at a pure and essential core, from which nothing further could be stripped away. Some students grew impatient, rejecting this stratagem, denouncing his pedagogical methods. In order to follow his thinking, Régnier's students had to agree from the start to step out onto precarious foundations and submit to a certain conceptual vertigo. During the last class, partially vindicating his detractors with a final middle finger, he came to the conclusion that a conclusion was impossible. What they were looking for was elsewhere. From one class to the next, over the course of this journey of privation, the students' very idea of absence, of lack, was reversed, overturned. And it was then that Régnier shared his precious idea, the final nail in the coffin.

The virus is not the viral particle,
that little box we use to describe our idea
of what a virus is.
A virus is what happens when it leaves the box and
enters the cell. A virus is a relationship.

It was all there already—the major original idea of his work, the initial intuition that would keep the kaleidoscope of thought turning, remixing and reassembling the same elements that were all already there.

This was how Sadie came to Science. Against the grain. She first encountered the structures and foundations of the discipline through their destabilization. A whole world of theory opened up to her in a state of seismic disequilibrium. But she'd accepted it; it was clear that she had already accepted all of it. She had no frame of reference by which to evaluate Régnier's method, but she was struck by the way his thinking was contaminated by its subject: he thought infectiously. She had never seen anything like it, the way he let his observations seep into the core of the very notions he needed to draw on to make sense of what he saw. A tightrope walker of the intellect.

In that grim classroom, where a few narrow windows—mere slits, really—looked out onto the interior courtyard of a rather carceral panopticon, Régnier created an opening to a dimension Sadie had never imagined, a minuscule world that evades our gaze and yet is swarming everywhere among us. In that rumble of the living, Sadie discovered a mode of thinking in which the concepts themselves came alive.

She wrote down everything she could manage to catch as he lectured, she took notes ardently, her notebooks becoming the archive of frequently incomplete sentences she'd spend the next decades meditating on, decoding. She wrote furiously, wanting to get it all down. But her notes, hasty and rushed, could never quite capture everything. Her notebooks—top quality, always impeccable, governed by a clear and efficient transcription system in which meticulous, irreproachable handwriting was carefully aligned and proportioned—gradually filled with barely recognizable letters, disfigured by the avidity of her mind. The fear of letting words slip by unrecorded intensified. She'd had this obsession since childhood, a preoccupation that had led to the development of her efficient transcription technique. But in Régnier's classroom, her system was of no help. This was something else, and it had to be contained. A new world of knowledge required a new language of gestures. As she wrote, she could glimpse in her peripheral vision the way her scribbles were sullying the beautiful pages of her notebook, but she didn't have time to linger over her uneven, and before long disgraceful, handwriting. Over the course of the semester, her movements intensified as she adapted to the unpredictable rhythm of Régnier's speech. Her hand grew less concerned with properly closing a letter's loops, it gained confidence, and she soon took a certain pleasure in the chaos of her poor handwriting.

Many of her classmates could not keep up. They sat silently in their seats, out of their depth. So it fell to her—she could keep up, she wouldn't give up—to record the high-wire act of ideas. Sadie had the growing impression that Régnier was speaking to her and her alone.

X

Despite having spent her formative years trying to wrap her head around conceptual structures, each one more complex than the last. Despite having lived, in the first years of her adult life, *inside* those abstract architectures, moving from one speculative fortress to another, sometimes by the official passages of History, other times hitting narrow dead ends, improvised crossroads. Despite all this.

Régnier's lectures thrust her into the realm of the living. The constructions she had explored and investigated were suddenly flattened. The whole structure that should have allowed thought to move to another order of reality, to move beyond the coarse, crude appearances of the common world—she suddenly realized that it was all going nowhere, that it was only responding to the need for thought to embed itself deeper and deeper inside more and more complex structures, producing an exponential quantity of concepts that were effective only in pushing disorder and chance outside its walls. In the Faculty of Philosophy, there was no possible escape from this deleterious world of illusions, but instead an ever more sophisticated system of compartmentalization.

When she thinks back to those days, Sadie tends to forget that she had in fact resisted that breakdown of her universe, seeking refuge for a time in ancient texts that seemed more relevant to the questions that were awakening in her. It was reassuring, for a time, to look back, to return to the beginnings of the philosophical tradition that had shaped her and search for something that might have been forgotten, left behind on the journey to rationality. Thales of Miletus, Anaximander, Heraclitus: she spent some time wandering through the strange and scattered remnants of their worlds and put that archaic knowledge, still all mixed up with the myths it was trying to leave behind, into dialogue with the new science whose language she was just now learning. Those thinkers who had lived on islands off the coast of what is now Turkey, where the solid world meets the liquid world, in an environment much more fluid than the desert that had given birth to our monotheistic traditions, did they not still have something to teach us? Was there not still a link between the study of life and the development of thought? Could she find a moment when philosophy had not been a defensive reflex against the unexpected?

It was too late for Antiquity. Within the drab green concrete walls of the university, as she discovered the moving complexity of the most basic structures of the living world, she realized how much mental energy she had invested from the very start of her education in pushing away the unpredictable, random nature of the sensory world. So much energy spent trying to extricate herself not only from what makes up every part of each one of us but also from what, at every moment, we are participating in.

Sadie never finished her studies in philosophy. She converted, at the age of twenty-five, to science. She abandoned the doctoral thesis she'd begun writing on the prophetic vocation of philosophy. She left philosophy and its moribund corridors, and she left many other things at the same time—her family, her city, her country. She did not answer the call of philosophy. She took another path.

X

That is what Régnier gave her. He made her see the sterile illusion to which she would have devoted herself. He was the first person in that cozy prison of ideas to offer something else. The concrete that she had once thought inert began to hum with innumerable life forms, millions of viruses, and bacteria, invisible particles. All that life had always been there, under her nose. In return, he recognized an awakening in her. She went to see him in his office and he made space for her. He took the time to walk her through the phenomena he was studying, of which the class received only a fragmented, condensed version. During their conversations, which quickly became informal, he hinted at the potential implications of his research, and soon his hypotheses too, sometimes even the rough ideas he was preoccupied with. He let her see the unfinished stage. She could tell that he was lonely. He would never have admitted it, but it stung to not be taken seriously, to be an outsider in his field. She slipped into that gap of pain. He hated them all, but the cycle of his resentment, in which he directed his contempt for his peers back at himself, didn't stop there. It kept the machine running, and it transferred to his research with an aggressive energy. She saw all of this. Régnier had a furious brilliance.

X

Sadie is not a philosopher. She put that call on hold, picked up another line. But she did hang on to that fable, from that period in her life, the time before she met Régnier, the fable from the history of ideas—the story of the three humiliations of humanity. The knowledge now taking shape in her, twenty-five years later, is not exactly the answer to a philosophical question, but she nonetheless has the impression of returning to a question whose limits she could not assign to any field of human thought. The next humiliation, the one she sees looming every day, will not, she thinks, arise out of the epiphany of a single mind, nor will it be embodied in the revolution that will bear its name. No, this humiliation originates with a very small life form, so small it is already here among us, already a part of our lives, muscling its way in every day, colonizing us, becoming a part of us.

If we are to believe the majority, it is a life form so small that it has no real place within the kingdom of the living. We use its name to speak of those we want to cast out of humanity. Parasites, we call them. Vulgar parasites.

But the parasite will soon have the last laugh. Sadie is there to bear witness. Every day, she goes to the laboratory and takes her place behind the microscope and vials, and every day she is witness to the spectacular life of viruses.

XX

When scientists discovered the first giant viruses, they weren't quite sure what they were looking at. These viruses were far too big and complex, while humans thought of viruses as small, simple, and threatening. What was discovered in the water of an industrial air conditioner in Bradford, England, could only be a bacterium, they thought, something far larger than a virus and which of course would have claim to the status of living being. For ten years, the specimen sat unseen right before the researchers' eyes until someone, one day, allowed their mind to think differently about what they were seeing. Up to that point, it had gone unnoticed, totally under the radar, hiding and circulating in obscure journals without making any waves—until the day when yet another person looked at that same thing but this time, thinking outside the language that had confined the virus to its small, simple box, they recognized an unknown giant. Monstrously large.

Discovery consists of looking at the same thing as everyone else and thinking something different. Régnier had this quote, attributed to Albert Szent-Györgyi, a Hungarian researcher and winner of the

Nobel Prize in Medicine, tacked to the wall above his desk. Next to it was pinned a Polaroid of the sea that could have been any sea, but that Sadie knew was taken at the mouth of the Tunquén River, south of Valparaíso.

X

To isolate a virus, you take a sample of earth and kill every living thing inside it. The virus is what survives the onslaught of antibiotics.

During a months-long expedition to collect samples along the central coast of Chile, Régnier and Sadie isolated a new specimen of giant virus. At first, they didn't realize what they had. They thought it was a member of a family one of their colleagues had already identified; they thought they were being good stewards of knowledge, building on that earlier work, expanding the scope of scientific language. They felt a quiet gratification as they collected the thing.

The sea is full of viruses, like all oceans, really; you can sometimes find up to ten million viruses in a single millilitre. But what they collected in a container full of sediment turned out to have no relation to the giant viruses that had already been named. In fact, it was unlike anything in the world that had a name. It was definitely a virus, but one that aligned with nothing we knew of viruses.

When the first giant viruses were discovered a few years earlier, the scientific community was forced to recognize that there were things in nature that were not consistent with the concepts that made up the building blocks of our knowledge of the minuscule.

But the specimen they were looking at that day on a boat anchored off the coast of Chile belonged to another order of things, for which no nomenclature existed. A virus whose virion, the box visible to our eyes, was shaped like an amphora. A gigantic virus, which the preliminary analyses they quickly made with the equipment on board revealed to have a genome far more complex than that of any other virus ever identified. But what left them in a state of shock, after the first sequencing was complete, was that the majority of the characters in its genetic code resembled nothing else known.

"This thing is huge," Régnier said. "It's monstrous. We've never seen anything like this. And look at that virion, it looks like an amphora. This is a real Pandora's box we're opening here, Sadie."

Pandoravirus. The virus had a name.

Sadie didn't think the name was a great fit. She could see the satisfaction on Régnier's face, derived in part from his witticism. She didn't want to take that away from him, she wanted to share in the celebration with the rest of the team. She never came around to the name, but in that moment, the excitement and astonishment and a certain inner tumult prevented her from putting her finger on what bothered her, her aversion was all mixed up in an anarchic confusion of feelings.

She thought about it often. Pandora, "the all-endowed." The first human woman, and a real bitch at that, molded from clay to be the ruin of man, to make him pay for the audacity of his knowledge. Régnier enshrined their discovery in that story. He wanted to excite the imagination, this was the defining moment of his career, and it would look good on the cover of *Science Magazine*. Sadie understood all of that, but the story of Pandora still left a muddy taste in her mouth.

In the days that followed, as they got ready to travel back to Marseille, an uneasiness gnawed at Sadie's guts, but she didn't manage to dissect it, she couldn't isolate the embarrassment she felt at the name Pandora from the broader, more generalized awkwardness of naming a new virus. Perhaps she should have argued, negotiated. And yet, she'd had no suggestions. How do you name something that presents itself as an enigma, that shows up to tell you about a life whose parameters you don't yet understand? As if it had been waiting there, inert, to be discovered, as if it had been waiting for us before it assumed its final form. As if it were our own creature, fashioned out of the sediments of the Pacific. *And he called this woman Pandora, because all they who dwelt on Olympus gave each a gift, a plague to men who eat bread.* Sadie was familiar with the resentment that drove Régnier. She thought about it once she was alone again, she came back to Pandora. How quickly she'd opened the box. There was nothing she could do about that wicked impulse, the gods and goddesses had made her that way, racked with unsavoury curiosity, a constitutive defect that would serve to unleash a plethora of evils. Sadie tried to look beyond the obvious and articulate the relationship between, on the one hand, the rage against mediocrity that motivated Régnier, and, on the other, Jupiter's punishment for the hubris of humanity. Pandora wasn't stupid, she'd barely lifted the lid and was trying already to clean up the mess. She understood that she would be in for it once people realized that it was her fault if there was illness, her fault if there was pain, death. Only hope was left in the jar. *The rest, countless plagues, wander amongst men; for earth is full of evils and the sea is full. Of themselves diseases come upon men continually by day and by night, bringing mischief to mortals silently.* Maybe there was still time to change his mind. The virus they were bringing back was far from a calamity for humanity; it was indifferent to us.

They worked in highly controlled and safe conditions, and always ensured that what they were collecting contained nothing pathogenic for humans. People already got tense when the subject came up.

She considered the analogy that had been created in Régnier's mind, a little too spontaneously. As the image of the virus was imprinting on his retina, it had taken a shortcut to the myth, and so there was already a path cleared, there was a memory that Sadie didn't recognize. There was a misunderstanding in the scene where Régnier decided on the name. What worried her was that none of the explanations she could come up with managed to calm her intestinal tumult, the anxiety that manifested for days in an irrepressible yet spectral urge to defecate. She tried to put things in perspective. Months at sea had turned her guts inside out. Her stubborn concern eventually faded, became indistinguishable from the vague and generalized discomfort she had learned to ignore.

And so began, not long after their return, an intense period of work. Now that they had found this thing, they had to understand what it was. Adapt their language to the shock of the new. They spent days and nights thinking, keeping the current of thought flowing from one brain to the other. They thought as they ate, they thought as they walked, they thought as they slept. They very rarely left each other's company, bringing their viruses with them wherever they went. To understand what they were seeing, they needed to be together. They needed to think by addressing someone who knew the extent of the problem. The time to present the virus to the world, and to defend the territory of their acquired knowledge, would come later, later they would stand before the rest of the scientific community, maybe even the whole world. But this moment was one of a shared language between the two of them. There was a blurring of boundaries between the laboratory, the apartment, and the street, between the spaces of the day and those of the night. Every place became the site of intense and intimate reflection.

They still work like that, although they will never again reach that same level of intensity. Today, they are still a two-headed work monster, they forge a kind of thinking that transcends individual languages while still retaining something of the translation. With Régnier, Sadie works toward a composite knowledge. When she was younger, she often wondered what she had to offer him, this man whose knowledge and experience vastly exceeded her own. But over the years, they developed an intellectual dance in which the question of the limits of her capacities and even her own intelligence ceased to matter. That's why she's still there. In the work of association, she is able to eclipse herself.

X

This new virus was so enigmatic and confronted them with such an unknown that the most logical explanation was immediately clear: it had to be something very rare. They returned to Marseille with this evolutionary stray, an exile that had forgotten to die. They called it *Pandoravirus salinus,* for the salt water in which they'd found it. They got down to work, setting in motion the sophisticated computer operation that performed the complete genetic sequencing. But then, a few months later, 15,000 kilometres away, in the fresh water of a pond behind the University of Melbourne building where they were attending a conference, they found it again, by complete chance. *Pandoravirus dulcis.*

Their first reaction was to chalk it up to a calculation error. They must have skipped a step in the DNA sequencing. They redid all the operations and compared the results. There were no translation errors between the genes and the proteins. If these proteins were unlike anything else, it was because these viruses' genes were unlike anything else. These specimens were no biological aberration, they belonged to what was probably quite a large family that was populating the Earth without our knowledge. This thing exploded all the measures at their disposal for understanding it, and it became clear that there was no longer any limit when it came to its size and complexity.

A real Pandora's box, Sadie.

X X

Régnier interrupts her. He comes into the lab, he's slept badly, you can see it in his bloodshot eyes. He hasn't been sleeping well lately. He had to go off his sleeping pills a few weeks ago because his insurance company didn't want to pay anymore. Apparently, they don't condone a whole lifetime of artificial sleep. His diet isn't great either, too many restaurants, and his breath is acrid. In an ideal world, he would rather not eat out, as it is, he only goes to one or two restaurants, where they know him and his idiosyncrasies. They reserve the corner table so he can put the necessary distance between himself and the other patrons. He has to isolate himself, both from scents, all the perfume people drench themselves in and the fragrances that exude from their pores and give him terrible migraines, and from the horrific, wet sounds of mastication, which provoke anxiety and aggression in him. Given the right conditions, dining out can be almost pleasant. He appreciates good service, he likes the way a relationship of mutual gratitude is established, he enjoys the care taken with his space. He is magnanimous toward the staff who, in return, show an understanding of his particular situation. Generally speaking,

Régnier prefers to deal only with people who are accustomed to his restrictions. He functions much better in a controlled environment.

When Sadie met him, twenty-five years ago, he hadn't yet learned how to precisely identify the irritants in his surroundings, and frequently found himself in disagreeable situations from which he could escape only by even more disagreeable means. Sadie, adept at the art of diplomacy, made apologies on Régnier's behalf, rearranging the truth to justify his abrupt withdrawal from a project or to excuse his departure without warning from a dinner that had yet to even begin. When Sadie discovered this talent in herself, she began to simply arrange the world around him. Régnier was forty-five at the time. He had just gotten tenure, had just barely begun to breathe a little within the social constraints of academic unsociability. He did not, however, know how to coexist with those who shared a pathological egocentrism that prevented them from functioning in any other work environment. Régnier suffered for years until he at last had his own lab, which allowed him to relegate his relationship with the university to an affiliation and avoid interacting with idiots except on absolutely essential occasions, that is, the kind of occasions at which he received honours, in cash or in kind.

With time, and with Sadie's help, he learned how to better recognize and control his triggers. As his reputation grew, so did his irritability, and they reinforced one another, weaving a kind of protective buffer around his person. As with most cantankerous people who have the means to pass off their difficult nature as a lifestyle choice, this gave him the aura of a defiant nonconformist.

The more he pissed off the institution, the more his colleagues hated him, and the more he rose in esteem. At a certain point, it becomes harder and harder to separate the infuriating from the admirable.

It's not exactly that Régnier has come to know himself better, but with age his senses have gained new acuity. He can now recognize, from among a wealth of stimuli, which element will cause which reaction and organize his life accordingly. Régnier is a vast black hole to himself, but the outside world reaches him through the fine-tooth comb of a discerning, paranoid sensibility. And like all paranoiacs, who can anticipate every possibility in a given situation, he always ends up being right eventually. Like a human weather station, he can feel disturbances coming. Time has taken nothing from him, his senses seem only to sharpen with the years. Feelings accumulate within him as if they were stored in an incommensurable database, continually perfecting the program. That almost inhuman precision has always made a strong impression on Sadie, who brings her own intelligence to Régnier's defensive atmospheric activity. She contributes her own data and observations to the program, helping fine-tune the system. She has validated the models, ensured the reproducibility of hypotheses. It was Sadie who brought Régnier's specific madness into reality, who made a scientific theory of it.

He was her professor first, then her supervisor when she migrated from one discipline to another. She knew that once she started down this path it would be difficult to turn back. But the decision was made, there had been no question that she would work with viruses, and only Régnier did that kind of work with that level of intelligence. It was a done deal. Régnier was the perfect excuse for the great escape she needed: he was a constant force of betrayal, he lived to flout the rules. Except, of course, for the rules he imposed himself. With Régnier, Sadie discovered a grammar of perjury. She imagined herself fleeing with him on a raft while everything behind them burned. Over the years, in an increasingly sedentary way, she began to occupy an intermediary space between him and the world. He counts on her to fend off the constant aggressions from the outside world. A silent agreement exists between them, based on the idea that Régnier allowed her to leave the place she came from. He offered her exile, which comes with a certain set of commandments. This has never been said in so many words, of course. What they devote themselves to, every day in the lab, is well worth the investment.

In those first years, when he was supervising her doctoral research, he gave her dozens of books, classics in biology and the history of science, which he considered foundational texts. Charles Darwin, Thomas S. Kuhn, William James, Erwin Schrödinger, Albert Szent-Györgyi. Régnier has a particular affection for unconventional intellects, he finds comfort in the exclusive community of eccentric and often difficult thinkers. He considers himself their heir. Sadie's encounters with these texts led her to the painful realization that her studies in philosophy had managed to educate her as if the twentieth century had never happened. Her readings opened a door to a parallel world she'd been unaware of until now. These scientific minds formed a line of succession that Régnier made coherent, the way they passed the torch in the work of articulating the seam between two worlds, the old and the new, paving the way to a modern vision of the world from which her university in Montreal had protected her as if from dangerous heresy. It was true that she had encountered that professor in undergrad, the only one who taught contemporary philosophy, who had told the story of the three humiliations. His courses, however, were primarily taken by students from other departments, most often literature. He was ostensibly tolerated as a marginal phenomenon within the faculty, a passing whim of fashionable thought. When he died, suddenly and prematurely, any talk of posterity was quickly nipped in the bud, and he was never spoken of again within the walls of the department. It was in one of his seminars that the germ of an idea for Sadie's PhD thesis had taken shape, a course shrouded in a certain darkness, where something indiscernible was stirring, and which had given her, if not specific ideas, the impetus of a direction. There was a poetry in the professor's speech that attracted Sadie even as it threw her off balance. When the time came to choose a supervisor for her graduate work, she considered that slightly enigmatic option, where unexpected perspectives seemed to await. In the spring of the final year of her master's, she tried to set up a meeting with him, but she was too late, he'd already left to spend the summer in Europe. She put it off until the fall, and at the end of August, the plane carrying the professor home from a conference in the US crashed. She chose instead an affable, reasonable, traditional man who tolerated Sadie's projects while reining in her ambition.

As Sadie dove into the readings Régnier gave her, she sometimes encountered a furtive trace of her late professor, a vague intellectual kinship. For fear of sullying the precious books, she photocopied long passages and annotated them copiously. She felt feverish at the discovery of sentences Régnier had underlined, always with an impetuous flourish. Each time she came upon that vivid, singularly explosive line in her readings, she felt for the first time that she was not alone. The marks that blackened the margins of these essential texts, sometimes encroaching on the printed words like furious metastases, made her a privileged witness to what had at some moment touched Régnier. Her attention was focused on these chosen excerpts: the more she read and the more time she spent with him, the more she began to recognize, in each sequence of words marked by his hand, the network of meaning that had been created in Régnier's mind. In his marginalia, she found a portrait of the intelligence that had been at work in his classroom lectures. Discovering his unique brilliance, his always unexpected point of view, the way he articulated contrasts, his analogies that made seemingly irreconcilable worlds suddenly exist together in a new idea—all of it made Sadie feel like life was transcending itself.

Most of the time, a glance at Régnier's handwriting was enough. Elsewhere, she went back over his lines, training her hand to replicate his nimble, almost vehement stroke.

X

Every morning, Sadie opens the door of the building, she walks up three flights of stairs, she enters the still-silent lab, pulls on her lab coat and gloves, and sits at her workstation. A bubble of silence forms around her as she bends over her microscope.

The microscope is no longer just a tool. It becomes an extension of herself, she gazes into it and, by the genius of refracted light, it reflects back everything that her human brain must forget at every moment in order to experience a coherent world. The microscope reconnects her to a visible world she must continuously dismiss from her mind in order to live. When she gets up again, a few hours later, when she straightens out her spine to step back into her human life, she will resume the process of forgetting, she will forget the life that surrounds her, the life that abounds inside her and all around, close by and far off into a distance she cannot even begin to imagine.

It is also a slowing down. Under the microscope, magnified life alters the nature of time. Seeing requires another temporality. Suddenly, she has time to see everything that the structure of her eye conceals each day as it adjusts the rhythm to its capacities. Out in the street, at home, beyond the microscope, she sees at her own scale. She would need infinite time to see the infinitely small, which would cause her to fall dangerously behind. She might never catch up to the human race again.

Only Régnier interrupts. Every day, at an unpredictable hour, the sound of the door jostles her nervous system and sends a short shock wave down her spine. She looks up, waves. Performs a quick assessment of his general state of being. Degree of tension in his facial muscles, rhythm of his movements, overall level of agitation. She then modulates her greeting based on her observations. This process, which she has perfected over the years, feeding it with an ever-greater quantity of data, requires no more than a few seconds and is for the most part automatic. When Régnier seems particularly on edge, she adapts her reaction, giving herself time to account for possible unknowns. But there are, in general, very few unknowns. Régnier is nothing but consistent in his inconsistency and so can be read without much difficulty; the regulatory control that ensues is exercised in a rather limited register. In short, her task consists of guiding his system back to a state of balance. Restoring a level of seeming neutrality to the interactions of his internal forces with the outside world. Helping him block out the noise, the anarchic racket of life that he finds so unbearable.

XX

She works six days a week, taking advantage of the quiet in the lab on Saturdays. Most Saturday nights, she goes dancing at Scum, when Molly is DJing. Alone on her little platform, Molly is a one-woman orchestra reigning behind her laptop and turntables. Sadie gives herself over to Molly's hands, which are made manifold. Molly knows how to create an atmosphere. At first, people are still chatting back and forth—"Yeah, it's finally getting warmer out, we needed this," "So when did you get back from Barcelona?" "Don't tell me those bastards didn't renew your contract"—the music just a background, allowing the neck and shoulders to relax, the jaw to unclench, all the tissues of the body to loosen. Molly knows how to start gently, how to encourage shoulder blades to float easily down the back, she knows just what's needed to discreetly infiltrate the dancers' bodies, the subtle bass notes, the core mobilizing and waking up, and before you've even realized it, the atmosphere has already pulled you in, the bass is pulsing inside you as a series of metallic, synthetic tonalities call on you to expand into the space. Molly has mastered the art of metamorphosis and the pleasure of the transition, moving seamlessly from one track to the next so that you find yourself already in it with no way of knowing how you got there. The apparition of the new is never violent, but an opening onto another intelligence, it doesn't need to be understood, just inhabited, and that intelligence of movement, vibrations, and waves welcomes the dancers, takes hold of their spines. Sadie feels the stiffness melt away from her vertebrae, her neck lengthens, in the distance Molly is visible in flashes, her sylphic, almost inhuman figure, neon-yellow hair, bright red lipstick, her whole body signalling irony, Molly is a poseur, always rewriting a morphology in space, and when she mixes, she becomes a conduit, the dancers catch only intermittent glimpses of her, now and again they forget to see her, and Sadie forgets a little too, her eyes become a secondary organ among infinite receptors, like millions of hairs swaying around her, collecting information indiscriminately, there is Molly, undulating in the distance, a long-limbed goddess, there is a strong scent of pot, voices moving from French to Italian, to Wolof, to Korean, to Kashmiri, voices from all the places Molly travels to collect her samples, often without leaving her desk, the eighth notes of a drum resound beneath the elastic, rubbery sound of a kind of mouth harp before coming into the foreground, the drum's skin slides us into the oblivion of the air that was still giving rhythm to the whole body only seconds earlier, the air, which was everything, now becomes stickier, clinging to muscles and blood as we slip from one world of sound to another, it is Molly's genius that allows it, that carries us into that oblivion and makes it possible for "us" to exist at all, right now, we live and die with the music over and over again in the space of one evening, we lose sight of the lives we lead outside of this moment, we can no longer see, the dancing bodies are nothing more than scansion, the heat rises and sweat streams from pores that dilate like pupils in the dark, skin that was cold colliding at the start of the night now absorbs contact, layers of skin like tongues, almost fluid, exhaling foul odours, folds and crevices turn inside out, propelling soiled particles into the air that has become perceptible, it reeks of filth, unwashed, indelible shit, and the budding fermentation of corporal yeast, skin and its inhabitants tasting one another but with a certain indifference, friction doesn't matter, friction is a new language among the people of Scum.

Bodies speak to each other of a pain that everyday life obscures, a pain for which there is no expression in human language, like a dull hunger, verging on distress. Countless signals are exchanged between individuals who pay little attention to them, the instability spreads, becomes attractive, dancers nearby flock to it, make the pain more powerful, it is that distress close at hand that keeps time now, an anguish breathes and finds at last its full magnitude.

Pain, normally kept at a distance by pity or numbness, is now conveyed in prodigious transmission, each person usually closed off by their wounds is instead opened up by them, the separation of the individual becomes labile, the interior cloister momentarily cracked open. These beings, who just hours earlier were still moving through the world knowing nothing of the suffering inside them, are no closer to understanding their pain, but they encounter it in this movement, in the midst of an improvised group that will know no tomorrow. In the language of friction, nothing is permanent, the bass never stops, it multiplies, it drives the night forward with its repetition, reinventing with every beat the glutinous, gluttonous body dancing.

XX

Sadie and Régnier fuck occasionally. It started at the university, an institution built on blurriness in the geometric translation of relationships. When she entered Régnier's space, she was surprised by a fervour, almost a fever, the opening up of a possibility that demanded investment. He had an office just like all the other offices that lined the identical corridors of the building's eleven floors. But the moment she stepped through its door, the quality of the space changed, and she herself was present in a different way, within those four walls she had seen countless iterations of. She walked into that enclosed space, and it was like entering a place where all her principles were suddenly called into question. Régnier gave off a challenging energy, he cultivated an anger that made the air around him tremble. That anger was intimately familiar to her, that hatred of everything around him, but she'd never before had a way to speak it. The only images of anger she'd inherited were blind explosions of rage, or else its suffocation in sterile rigour. In Régnier, she found a stylistics of loathing, a way to make something of her pain and send it back out into the world.

The disjointed pieces of her reality collided, and there was dis-comfort there, but also great excitement, and she didn't spend much time trying to identify its causes. The university buildings where she reported day after day continued to sit in a row like blocks of concrete dropped there by an entity completely devoid of imagination or mythology. Nowhere during the years of her education had she been able to find a threshold, a differentiation. When a new space appeared all of a sudden to tear open this tedium, she rushed into it.

There was certainly an element of disgust in all the tumult, from the very beginning, but she was too out of breath to pay attention to that beginning. Régnier made her chase him, he took every precaution, he was looking out for his career. This was centuries before girls started speaking out at school, but he was a trailblazer in that respect too. The professor must never make the first move, he said. This was his guiding principle, the categorical imperative in his science of interhierarchical fucking. He let the chase go on a long time to be sure he wasn't misreading a signal. But she was twenty-five years old and light on her feet. He didn't make a move himself until she had first compromised herself with an explicit proposition as bold as it was potentially humiliating. The asymp-tote of a possible misunderstanding dwindled until no margin of error remained. Then, at a mixer for students and profs, they found themselves in a corner of the room together. And there, in the late afternoon light shining in at an angle that left no room for ambiguity, his face appeared to her, Régnier's face, glistening with oil and pitted with pockmarks, the remnants of a teenage ugliness scarring the face she had until then seen only at a certain distance. It was as if all of a sudden some vestige of an awkward childhood was resurfacing in this larger-than-life character. She could have left; she recoiled and she could have let her aversion guide her. But she stayed. And she's still there, working with him. Sex is one of the languages in which her life continues within Régnier's life.

A few other prospects had offered her a way out of her relationship with Régnier, which she'd quickly realized had the potential to drain her energy. On several occasions, she glimpsed another path in the eyes of one of those young men, full of unblemished hope, as beautiful as they were unbearable in their belief that everything was still possible, that they were meant for greater things. But she didn't take that fork in the road. She was tempted a few times to join them, to contemplate through their eyes the other paths of life still open to her. But instead she stayed the course, full speed on the highway, full speed with Régnier. Today, she can see that this choice allowed her to escape the relationships that would have led her to the dead end of a quiet existence, or, worse, fulfilled. Her relationship with Régnier cured her first of any yearning for coupled life, and eventually of any aspiration to any form of interpersonal satisfaction.

She spent the rest of her time with the viruses, and with other bodies that were not Régnier's. She'd started sleeping with women relatively late, around thirty-five. At that point, she already had her ideas about coupledom, and she'd already made peace with her expectations for what another person might bring to her life. She would never have arrived at this other sexuality if she'd settled into a vaguely satisfying relationship with a man that wasn't Régnier, if she'd committed to some traditional relationship that was more or less good for her, adhering to the limits of the pleasure principle. Before her first experiences with bodies that were not strictly masculine, she was convinced that she had grown up in an era that had shaped her permanently in the mould of heterosexual desire. At university, she'd hung out with a few full-on lesbians, but it seemed too big a leap for her, too heavy a commitment. She had missed out on too much, in terms of the primary need for affection and security, to completely renounce the assurance, however illusory or compensatory, promised by the narcissism of the cock.

While she still sometimes sleeps with an old fart like Régnier, while her desire still sometimes expresses itself like that, it is increasingly rare, and out of habit more than interest. She recognizes the mechanics of that pleasure. She gets off on the gap between their ages, the disgust she still feels for Régnier creates a discrepancy and magnifies her image of her own body. Her femininity has grown more and more strange to her, like a kind of parody. She has no imagination, so the feminine, to her, is about smooth curves, marked contrasts between firm and soft, represented by the generally accepted images of hardness and abundance, while leaving her own body to drift in a growing blur in which the question of gender is less and less resolved. When she was younger, the fantasy didn't clash too badly with reality, it seemed a simple exaggeration, a filter to enhance bodies. As her body starts to show its years, it doesn't fit quite as well; she's forced to see the places where the fantasy doesn't hold up. Régnier's aging male body is in the process of becoming frankly disgusting, but he doesn't have the slightest idea, and that detachment from reality, the persistent negation of his own consistency, allows Sadie, in very brief moments, to get off on an interposed image. He allows her that hallucination. He will always have been that disgusting body for her, but his lack of awareness created a mis-understanding from the very beginning, which found a way to persist. Régnier has always been mistaken about himself, but it's as true now as it was twenty-five years ago. He maintains the abil-ity to freeze himself in time. To create in the formaldehyde of his memory the infinite potential for repetition.

X

With other bodies too, there was and sometimes still is disgust. She can't forget it completely. She did try to see it like a threshold that she was crossing, at the border of the masculine and the fem-inine. She tried to see in it an act of renunciation of everything she'd known and practised before. After all, knowing how to leave was part of who she was. But now she can no longer pinpoint a first time, a first woman. And with age, she's become less and less sure of how to situate herself, her own body, on the scale of fem-ininity. She hadn't asked herself the question when she was younger, when so much depended on context. The younger gen-erations have since come of age with a pressing need to precisely situate each person on the spectrum of fluidity. She often sleeps with younger people, and their confusion suits her as much as it irritates her. She came to know those bodies, made up of so many mucous membranes, that pliable skin that makes her heart lurch, her lips curl, in that instant that no longer holds the attraction of aversion. In their crimps and folds, inverted and inside out, turning over and around again, everything starts to blur, her heart spinning, blood rushing to her cheeks and then running cold, she flows and ebbs, the fluids curdling in her stomach, her guts churning, she can taste it, rolling in her mouth, flesh meeting flesh, everything is too slippery, too slimy, she read somewhere about the obscure role intestinal peptides play in the swelling of the vaginal membranes, the oxygenation of their secretions, it's still fuzzy, scientific language can only roughly follow the nebulous course of fluids—*it is glaringly obvious that we know so little*—from one tissue to another, from one cell to another, as it creates proximities, improbable exchanges between organs. Knowledge is generated among the cells, the peptides, the molecules in the vagina and those in the intestine, and the heart, and the brain, but soon knowledge outstrips the organism, there is too much fluid for the cells to absorb—this whole process is overdue for more in-depth experimental investigation—no one can explain its consistency, what makes it so slippery, she could lose all her senses in it, she could spill over, it's dangerous, for Sadie. Even today, it's still a dangerous feeling.

Abstraction is no longer possible in those bodies, the way mucosa meets mucosa. She encounters this flesh anew, and it allows her no perspective, she has her face stuffed inside it, mouth open, and it's there she must live for a time. She did try—to keep a distance, to sidestep, circumvent the uneasiness she feels being so terribly close to another—she tried, during the first few years, to move toward an epicentre that would invert the hideous countenance so she could finally see its beauty. Turn the slippery cleft into a monster with two faces, articulate her disgust in the first moment of reversal, confronting the revolting grimace and turning it over to see its hidden face. But she could never make it cohere into a new dialectic. She never managed to overcome that moment of unmanageable ambivalence once and for all, when revulsion rushes in and inundates her veins and her arteries, releases everything that is conducted through her, floods her mouth with an ancient metallic taste that is impossible to digest.

Afterward, she forgets, begins again. She can't summon up a single event that would have brought her across to the other shore, that would have made her say: it's much better over here anyway. It's a web, a kind of net secreted by each connection, each relationship replaying the whole. The bodies that come close shake up the network, send vibrations through its fabric: a grid stretched out over the possibilities of the body.

X X

When she gets home from the lab at night, Sadie takes a shower, eats a few quick bites, and picks up one of the three or four books— novels and essay collections—piled on her nightstand.

When she left philosophy and everything else in her life behind, she took only the books with her to guard against the brain dehydration she saw in her colleagues, brilliant scientists who read nothing but the so-called literature of scientific journals. Reading, for them, means *Science Communication, Nature Journal, Virology Studies.* Something hardens in them, their capacity for imagination shrivels up. They look at the world and are capable only of reproducing and applying the existing schematics. It becomes harder and harder to surprise them, as their mind loses its flexibility. Their neural activity is concentrated in the same main pathways and soon transits only through the major highways of thought. Books, however, are always carving out side roads. They train her to remain flexible to different routes and passages in the event that one day she might need to read something different in the world than what she normally reads. Her books prepare her to change course.

Paradoxically, it's often those who suffer from a chronic lack of originality who believe themselves to be utterly original. Each new experience, every reaction outside the ordinary, leaves them convinced that this is the first time in the history of humanity that someone has found themselves in that situation. Literature gives Sadie this too, it reminds her that her life is not reinventing life, that her feelings are nothing more than a variation on feelings already felt, which someone else has already taken the time to articulate. Reading gently reminds her of the banality of her existence.

As she reads, the parasites swim back into her mind, insinuating themselves between the letters on the page. In her reading, she betrays them. She returns to an interpretation that denies their existence. She must silence them to allow the sentence to take shape. Neurologists understand that reading is nothing more than the repurposing of an ancient neuronal system in the human brain, one that was initially intended to recognize visual shapes in the shapeless magma that surrounds it. Before us lies a world of visions, sounds, countless stimuli. Our survival depends on our ability to make order out of this constant assault of information, our ability to make sense of the world. We think we look around and see familiar faces and things, and even when we encounter something unknown, we perceive it as an object. But that perception is already the result of a complex process. Before we see and recognize objects for what they are, they are shapes, surfaces, outlines, borders, and contrasts appearing in different contexts, in perspectives that shift with each of our movements, or each of theirs. Our brains have learned to organize that chaos and to detect the recurring themes within it—to read reality.

The microscope thrusts Sadie back into a world in which the ability to read cannot be acquired definitively. In the microscopic world, she has to learn again how to find her way in her gaze, how to understand what appears before her. We often don't know how to read what we see. We are illiterate, without the language to name things. That is how the vast majority of viruses continue to go unnoticed, tiny things slipping through the sieve of human perception. Until the day someone leans over, crumples up their spine against the process of humanization, crouching down until they lose their language.

The parasites won't leave her alone. Sadie spends the whole day among them and by evening they're back, inhabiting her perception. The parasitic formations she examines all day remain in her vision, like in that optical illusion where you stare at a black spider on a white background for ten seconds and then look at the ceiling and the spider appears. They pop up here and there on the page, deforming a letter, forcing her eyes to focus and refocus again and again to not lose her place. As if beneath the characters that comprise the writing another form of reading was still ongoing in her head, a primitive reading for which she knows neither the code nor the grammar.

In nearly every alphabetical system created by human societies, the earliest shapes of the letters bore some resemblance or had some analogous relationship with the surrounding world. As those characters evolved, and in the gradual movement that brings them together, arranging these conglomerations in a sequence which, through a general process of recognition, are given a linear form—what we now call a sentence—there has always been an ancient need to assign order to the complex and dynamic visual chaos of all the things bustling around us. Our eyes must tirelessly convert what is shapeless to the regime of the shape. Through the reinvention of that primitive, formalizing compulsion, literature was born.

Parasitic life would have her unlearn how to read, which is why Sadie has to remember to always keep it at a bit of a distance. Every night, she relearns to read, she focuses, she fights against a kind of primal confusion. She attempts to put the viral particles under house arrest in their petri dishes and containers, neatly lined up in the refrigerated units of the secure areas of the lab on the fourth floor of the university centre. But the hum of the living sneaks in through the figures that take shape, through the metaphorical links, the bundles of letters, and she can never completely escape the sensory swarming.

X X

Headphones on, Sadie is deep in her microscope, inside a bubble that vibrates to the rhythm of the last playlist Molly sent her. She taps out the beat in Vivien Goldman's "Laundrette" and then skips to Stereo Total's "Troglodyten," going underground to forget the law of the sun for a little while.

Molly sends her playlists and Sadie doesn't even look at the artists. There's rarely anything familiar. She needs a musical environment to work, to isolate herself from the rest of the world, but she has no curiosity, neither the inclination nor the energy to seek out new sounds for herself. She enjoys making her way through other people's tastes. This is the tacit agreement she has with Molly, who passes on her discoveries, stringing them together to create little sensory wonders, she knows exactly what Sadie needs to concentrate, even if Molly never thinks of it that way, she never thinks of Sadie when she creates a playlist. Sadie settles into the indifference that brushes past her just as she would slip into another person's clothes, another person's skin. Molly is the ideal dealer of sound, something not everyone can do. It takes both basic selfishness and infinite generosity to know how to give the most central desire. A DJ who tries to please other people is useless, they'll bomb every time. You're either a dealer or you're a whore, you have to choose. Molly only passes on her best shit, the stuff that gets her high. She's not the slightest bit interested in other people's desires. Sadie infiltrates that high, slips into those underground passages carved out by a curiosity she lacks. She gets her fix by entering someone else's home through the keyhole.

Molly lends herself perfectly to this tendency. There's a certain amount of resistance, however; she is not infinitely accessible. When she senses Sadie is grasping a little too greedily at the eccentricity she so painstakingly cultivates, Molly knows how to pull back. She enthusiastically pours herself into others as long as it's mostly derivatives, jealously guarding the core of her originality, always remaining somewhat unavailable. Sadie reaches her only through her explorations, by donning second-hand the stylistic creations Molly leaves trailing in her wake. That's all there is to love about Molly, the fictions she produces. Molly is much younger than Sadie, somewhere in her thirties, but Sadie wants to adopt everything about her, all the images she creates to survive. The sovereignty she invents for herself, and which she must reconstruct every day, with grand declarations of independence to all those she shares herself with. Born into a Scandinavian culture that considers standing out a shameful vice, Molly came here to live out her desire to shine in the sun. Sadie agrees to love this, to accept her share and then a few extra crumbs. Molly has a penchant for younger people who are equal parts ambitious and lazy and, to Sadie's chagrin, she is blindly indulgent of the particularly intractable streak of mediocrity generated by this combination.

Sadie embraces her inconsistencies and handles her occasional train wrecks, when Molly is dumped by a drug-addled heiress or a histrionic filmmaker. Even when she's bogged down in the deepest despair, Molly still produces the most beautiful trash.

When she shows up mid-disaster to crash at Sadie's place for a few days, Molly sleeps next to her in bed but they never really touch, or only by accident. Sadie understood early in their friendship that they wouldn't go there. Molly takes over a space immediately; when she crashes at Sadie's, she settles in like the apartment was waiting for her. She doesn't hesitate before sinking into the only comfortable chair or messing up the kitchen. Molly fills the place with sound according to her mood. Fascinated by this convex form of life, Sadie gives in before she can even get annoyed. She can only admire Molly's ease of movement through the world, and her expansive presence releases her from something Sadie can't exactly name. She keeps her cool and picks up what Molly leaves lying around, she appropriates her leftovers, her leather jacket, her haircut, her dejected look, her rolled cigarettes, the details of her gestures. Sadie takes care of her while she puts herself back together. She plays it carefully. If she goes too far, Molly will freak out, but as long as Sadie doesn't cross the line and contents herself with quietly gobbling up the remnants, Molly will still feel like she is sharing without compromising herself.

There's something indecent about it, an older woman mimicking her younger friend like this, something unnatural about the transmission flowing in this direction. But Molly's understanding of the world is musical first and foremost, and so for her, the passage from one place to another, from one person to another, is anything but chronological. Places, like geographic zones, are organized by networks of influence, intersections; sound circulates, and is collected, and transformed. The metamorphosis of musical material simultaneously creates networks in time. Molly travels between continents and eras, concocting encounters between the elements, where space and time lose their usual consistency.

X

While Sadie's experience of the viruses is all wrapped up in this sonic universe, the viruses know nothing of sound waves and vibrations. They live in another environment altogether, they don't know about heartbeats, they don't know about blood flow, they are not born of the brutality of the flesh. And yet, they live. Sadie is convinced of it, even if she cannot quite pinpoint what makes her so certain. "Convinced," "certain"—the words are still too human to describe how this life communicates, whispering to her each day. When Sadie tries to touch that life with language, the idea falls apart.

When she gets close to the virus, when she puts her eye to the keyhole and loses sight of everything else, the whole logic on which her understanding of the world is based begins to buckle. She needs to hang on to some concept or category to not lose her bearings. So she holds onto a few words, for a minimum of guidance, to keep some sense of what it is to inhabit the world as a human. She measures, she refers to invariables, she makes lists, she speaks in graphs.

What she observes, what they call *Pandoravirus dulcis, Pandoravirus salinus,* is only the viral particle, the little box in which the virus can be seen. We name what we can delimit and define. And no notion of the living may answer to this name. The virus is not alive: a large part of the scientific community is committed to defending that fundamental idea, the guardians of the kingdom are particularly virulent on this point. A living thing reproduces. A living thing procreates. A living thing expands, grows with time. A living thing metabolizes energy. A living thing produces offspring.

Meanwhile, they say. A virus cannot reproduce itself. A virus has no offspring. A virus does not give life, it only receives it. It has neither ancestors nor descendants. Before it encounters the cell, it is completely inert. The virus infects the cell and takes over its reproductive mechanism to produce copies of itself. A proper hijacking, the virus preying on the irreducible structure of life. The invader instates a simple but effective regime of occupation. Once inside the cell, the virus has almost nothing to do, because the other thing is that it's lazy. A good occupying force, reassuring, promising a smooth transition: oh no, don't change a thing, keep doing everything you were doing before, we're still running the same program, we're just going to change the production a little, you'll see, everything will go smoothly. Viruses just live off beings who are gifted with life. They're nothing more than fucking trolls of the living. That's what the guardians of knowledge say.

It needs a cell. Alone in its little box, the virus is nothing but an assembly of molecules. It's passive, completely subject to its environment. Humans inevitably reach for human logic to understand the virus, and it's easy, the figure of the parasite is right there, ready and waiting.

Nothing more than a dirty parasite.

Régnier comes into the lab. He's irritated, that's obvious, his nostrils flaring in rapid, nervous twitches. Sadie has her headphones on but doesn't need the soundtrack to know that he is breathing in short, irregular jerks, two or three quick, bracing inhalations followed by a single, more powerful exhalation. A fragrance. Cologne. The new intern is wearing cologne. Régnier has tracked it across the room. Sadie pulls off her headphones and leaves her viruses. She gets up and goes over to soothe the intern Régnier is already interrogating.

"You were specifically told in your interview, and it was reiterated in your contract. Scents give me terrible migraines. And what is that awful stench anyway? Versace? Givenchy? It's Givenchy, isn't it? There's nothing more odious than Givenchy..."

"It's...Guerlain...It...it was a gift...," says the intern, trailing off as his face drains of colour.

"Ah, Guerlain! I knew it! Foul stuff. You'll have to go home and wash it off, this won't do at all. I'm already not going to make it through the day."

Sadie leads the trembling intern out of the lab and calmly explains the facts. She has a protocol for these types of situations. The more he unravels, the firmer she becomes; she speaks slowly, articulating her words precisely.

"He's very allergic, he's hypersensitive to scents…which means chemical products, yes, but it can even be flowers. Did you know that florists add artificial perfumes to flowers? They coat the petals in it, and, of course, some flowers are also just naturally more aggressive than others. Anyway, you'll see, you'll get used to it, we all do. It becomes a habit."

She sends the intern home with a measured degree of empathy, tells him to work on the article for *Nature Communications*. "Okay? So we're all set, see you tomorrow."

It's true, they all get used to it. It's been years since Sadie started using only neutral, unscented products around Régnier. Over time, she weeded out her bathroom cabinet. Being sniffed trained her to ensure she was completely odourless. Even unscented products still sometimes had a scent, that was another lesson. She gives a lot of brand-new products to Molly when they don't pass the sniff test. When she sees Régnier's nose start to twitch, his nostrils flare in little jerks, the investigative sniffs followed by an exhalation that's more like a spasm than a breath, her own system is triggered. She starts to sweat, she tries to locate the source. All the recalcitrant technicians, all the repeat-offender students she had to dismiss, she's lost track. The scent of lotions, deodorants, hair gel, laundry detergent, aftershave. Women and men both. Régnier maintains a ruthless but democratic contempt for delinquents. High status won't get you off the hook, there's no such thing as a minor infraction.

In the secure microbiology station where the virus is kept, they are able to control most factors of their environment. Since Sadie spends most of her time in the lab, and therefore with Régnier, she has learned to aim for neutrality for herself. She is careful that nothing escapes the impermeable seal of her headphones, she rounds her edges, she makes herself melamine. The current reverberates off the internal walls of her human envelope and creates a flow of intensity that only Régnier interrupts.

XX

She does, however, maintain a few zones of exception. When Sadie goes out dancing at Scum, she wears as much perfume as possible. She drenches herself in it, bathing her skin in sickly sweet fragrances macerating in flashy bottles. This is her only luxury. She sprays a mist of chemicals into the air and lets it rain down on her. She also takes a heavy hand with her makeup. Refuses to choose between lips and eyes. It pushes the limits of vulgarity at her age, verging on skanky, the old tart; the word that spontaneously comes to mind is *cagole*. It fills her mouth with a bad taste, something hyperlocal, the taste of petty crime. Marseille has given her new words, a whole other language; when she speaks, she feels the full force of a life that would not have been available to her in Quebec. The words remind her that she has the ability to don a whole new set of clothes, and when she does, she goes all out. Régnier never sees her on these nights out.

Scum is owned and operated by Veronica. She left the Brazilian coast in her twenties to remake her life and her body. She lived in New York for a few years, working as a bartender, and left the continent when it got too expensive. That was where she transitioned, leaving behind the unhappy boy people knew, and New York became the tomb of the pain she'd carried in that body. When she landed in Marseille in the mid-nineties, she was resolutely elsewhere. Veronica hated Paris and she couldn't take the cold anymore, not since the shock of New York winters that had chilled her to the bone. In Marseille, she found something like Rio, a filth, a charge in the air, a hard, dirty life in the heat. Virility too, but she now saw that from another angle. She is ogled as she walks down the street in Noailles, she feels their thirst roll down her neck, down the curve of her body, she knows she could always defend herself if it came to that, she still carries the reflex of violence in her nervous system, but she knows that culture from the inside, she grew up inside that hunger, she knows its choreography. And in those voices sticky with the sun, in those lingering looks, Veronica replays a scene she saw so often in Rio, but this time she's cast in the role she has chosen. Marseille lets her be the Brazilian woman she could never have been back home. Where some see scum, the dregs of society, she recognizes the style of the place she comes from. The guys she sees hanging around the cafés in Belsunce are her brothers, the merchants in Noailles her uncles, her aunts, her parents.

And she also came for the sea. She lives pressed right up against it, looking out onto its expanses with her back to a country that will never be hers, but she doesn't care because the city belongs to a much larger community, Marseille is Mediterranean first, and only French long after. Here, Veronica's accent is no longer South American, as it would be in Paris or Lyon, here her accent is also from Corsica, Tunisia, Casablanca, Tripoli, Tel Aviv,

Antalya. On her days off, she goes out on her friend Orphée's boat, they drop anchor off Frioul or in a calanque for the day. At twilight, as the setting sun gives the rocks a chalky texture, when the air around her settles into a pastel softness unlike anything on dry land, Veronica nestles into the hollow of a story she knows intimately even though nobody ever told it to her, a story of seafarers. She imagines that she will never return to shore, letting herself float on the surface, she tells herself that she will leave with Orphée on the *Libertad*, they'll live from port to port, she'll be nothing more than a resident of the seas. Orphée became a sound engineer after leaving his job as an archivist, fed up with spending his days in dusty silence, and he's still trying to carve out a place for himself, that's how he and Veronica became friends, she knew his twin sister Gitta, he started offering her free repairs for the system at Scum, and since she knows everyone, Veronica gets him contracts that allow him to maintain his intermittent worker status.

There is something touching about Orphée, with his stooped shoulders, life weighs on him, he is hollowed out by sadness in a way that's obvious from a distance. Orphée's twin sister died a few years ago, breast cancer found too late, he took care of her in her final months, a very painful but also very gentle time, as Veronica tells it, he accompanied his other half toward her death, when she could no longer walk he carried her onto the sailboat they'd inherited from their father, a Jewish-Hungarian refugee after World War II, wrapping her in warmer and warmer blankets into the heat of August, wrapping her in his own skin when she had nothing left to protect her from the life of pain that refused death. The brother let the sister—made greedy, hungry for life by the perpetual warfare within her—eat up his energy, his health, he gave her all his living strength, he drew on his last reserves to nourish the great activity of her final act. Sadie hadn't known Gitta, had only seen photos of her on social media, but Veronica, who'd been her close friend, told Sadie how, in the work of dying, Gitta became a sort of queen, with a kingdom unto herself, which her own life was destroying as she insisted on living beyond her means. She never wanted to talk about her cancer as an evil invasion that was eating away at her and colonizing everything she had. She spoke of her illness as an activity that concerned her alone, a most intimate process, and at the same time, a kind of job—far from grieving her own life, she was working to live on inside the person with whom she'd shared her first blood, the person she'd known before knowing hunger, and who now gave himself to the fervour of her final appetite.

Sadie hadn't known Orphée while Gitta was still alive, she only knew him devastated, already delivered to death. When she goes out on his boat, she watches him shuffle along, handling the lines with a tired grace, and she can't help but see in his hollow form the fossil of his magnificent sister. Thin, nearly bald, he still has a moving beauty. Sadie believes she can see a trace of Gitta in his deep black eyes. When he throws himself into the water, Sadie has the feeling he is finally giving in to the weight that seems to be constantly pulling him toward the depths. When his body slices through the waves, there's a moment when she doesn't expect to ever see him resurface. Every time Veronica invites her to spend the weekend on the boat, Sadie accepts, telling herself that a little time away would be nice. And every time it's the same thing, she gets violently seasick and can think only about returning to dry land. She doesn't complain, she just looks for a fixed point on the horizon and waits for it to be over. Despite her queasiness, she appreciates the slow hours with Orphée and Veronica. It soothes her to watch Veronica drifting on the waves, her tall form like a scrap of paper floating and puckering in the water.

X

Veronica has a deep love for Valerie Solanas, and named her bar in her honour. Few people in Marseille are familiar with the woman who shot Andy Warhol in the stomach, and for those that do know about her, that's generally the extent of their knowledge. "Is Solanas the one who wanted to kill all men?" For Veronica, Solanas is so much more. Solanas is a lifestyle, a way of thinking. *Canaille* thinking, she says. Veronica loves that word. *Canaille*. From the Italian for a pack of dogs. We're dogs, Veronica says. We live like dogs, Sadie. She knows it isn't true, that Sadie lives in a comfortable apartment, that she lives a pretty standard bourgeois life, not a *canaille* life, rough and rakish. But for Veronica, none of that counts. That's what scum is to her.

She says: "You're a dog too, Sadie. You're vermin. You work like crazy for this Régnier asshole, and at the end of the day it's his name that will live on."

The way Veronica sees it, everyone who comes to dance at her bar is looking for somewhere they feel welcome, no matter where they come from, no matter what kind of life they lead by day or what kind of costumes or skins they wear, when night falls and they step into her bar to join the community of sound, they become scum. Veronica says that Scum is not a dogma, it's the opposite of dogma. In her bar, everyone comes together, no questions asked, on big nights when Molly is mixing, the place is teeming with people, bureaucrats mingling with the unemployed. Veronica welcomes everyone who wants to escape their daily life, everyone who wants to hop off the hamster wheel of their nine-to-five, to let it all go, everyone who doesn't want to take it out on the weak anymore, she welcomes them all into this place that is not her home, where nobody is the landlord. We are all renting a little plot in this life, Veronica says. She invites them into the night where everyone can cast off the chains they wear and the chains they hold. She says welcome to the bosses, the rapists, the wife-beaters, the accomplices, the informers, let them slum it, let them come and dance to the vermin beat. That, Sadie, is how we're going to change the world, Veronica says, by showing the powers that be what it feels like, to come undone in the dance of the underworld. Valerie Solanas gave Veronica a framework for thinking from the depths of the sewers she'd been confined to by different communities. Life had done some serious damage to Solanas, but she had managed to draw intellectual strength from it. Veronica says that we didn't heed her call, the call of scum. That Solanas was taken for a psychotic halfwit. And that it suits us just fine to believe that only madness can push a woman's thoughts of revolt all the way to murder.

In the nineties, Veronica had hung around with a crowd of intellectuals in New York, radical feminists who wanted to keep Solanas's message alive. But Veronica was always suspect in their eyes. Her love for Valerie would never be enough, she would always be a double agent to them. Veronica suffered a great deal, there was nowhere she was welcome, it was almost the death of her. That's why when she arrived in Marseille it was a matter of survival for her to create her own scum space, her own place, which would welcome anyone who wanted to change the system, even if only for one night. The sewers are open to anyone who wants to go down there and forget the laws of the sun for a while, she says.

At night, Veronica is no longer Brazilian, no longer trans, no longer a body that has had to withstand all that pain. Veronica is proud scum, dancing.

X

Sometimes, walking home alone from Scum, Sadie comes across a pack of rats. In Montreal, she would only ever glimpse rats by accident before they scurried back off into the darkness. They were barely distinguishable from slightly chubby mice. Montreal rats have to survive the winter, it's a hard life, it humbles them. They generally rely on proximity to restaurants, leaving the houses full of cats to more discreet mice. When Sadie was in her teens, it was her job to knock out the rats that would flood into the basement on days of heavy rain. Her father would hand her and her brother a shovel or a broom, and the three of them would go downstairs in their rubber boots and hunt rats. She learned that rats are not easily killed, they can hang on a long time. Thankfully, the presence of humans brandishing weapons was usually enough to make them scuttle away.

Nothing had prepared her for this. A dozen rats as big as cats comfortably tucking into a feast of garbage. In her disgusted surprise, prolonged by the lack of reaction on the part of the rats, Sadie realized that they were waiting for her to scurry off, she was the bystander from a derelict species. The image stayed with her, the arrogance of the rat people.

X X

One afternoon in September, Sadie is alone in the lab. Régnier is at a conference in Munich. The lab is on one of the university's campuses situated between the city and the Calanques. After work, Sadie often goes down to walk along the rocks through a landscape that still impresses her. Familiarity has never dulled her response. She takes a path that passes beneath the old oak trees planted there two centuries ago. The oaks are an anomaly, the only survivors of a settlement by rich landowners who domesticated the land in the hopes of making a hostile natural landscape less threatening. The oaks kept growing, and some died and were never removed. Lizards feed on the insects that proliferate in the decaying wood, a strange, imported windfall for soil that had never expected such a feast.

From the campus to the sea, Sadie follows the path of vegetal evolution in reverse, from the fragrant pine forest to the brush invaded by rosemary, then the rocks where only tough grasses grow. Even after so many years, she is overcome by the powdery, almost dusty look of these rocky expanses, as if the colours have been sanded down. She found this soothing when she first arrived here, coming from a place that always felt too bright, a nervous landscape that renewed itself each season to continually assault the senses with overly luxuriant greens, or an orgy of reds and oranges, or a sparkling white that stung the eyes. The people who live there are constantly blinded, Sadie thinks, tormented by nature.

When she first landed in Marseille, Sadie felt like someone had wrapped all her senses in cotton wool, she could finally hear herself think after a lifetime of constantly tense nerves. On the bus that brought her from the airport to Saint-Charles station, a route she takes every time she returns from one of her trips with Régnier, she felt that release for the first time, in this place that seemed prehistoric, a place that had nothing to do with her and nothing to tell her about herself. The mountains, formed from the sediments of bodies from an era long before her own, spoke to her in the language of the sea. The North American murmur of a too-close, too-recent past, constantly trying to plug the leaks of another, more distant past that it attempts to repress, suddenly gave way to a vaster expanse of time, in which she could finally hear herself think. She'd arrived in the middle of August, into an extreme, dry heat that had gently engulfed her, promising to release her from the overwrought weather of Montreal, which barely thaws out from the cold before being plunged into an oppressive, suffocating humidity.

But while she can still feel that calm as she walks down toward the Calanques on this September day, it has never permanently settled in her, it's often disrupted by another sensation, the feeling of a sharp ridge among the ancient rocks that wants to split the flesh of the present. There remains something barbed in this antediluvian calm, and it demands her attention, as if she might inadvertently slice open her foot on its jagged edge.

On her way back up toward the lab, as an impossible mistral sweeps away the heat, Sadie stops for a moment in the shade of an oak that has stood up to the wild winds for many years. Just as Régnier would do if he were there, she bends to gather a bit of soil from the foot of the tree. Régnier has this almost poetic habit of halting mid-walk—guided by a clue, an intuition, some disruption indiscernible to the common man—and taking a sample. A rather routine act for a researcher in his field, but he gives it a mystical, almost witchy quality, as if performing a ritual whose methods had been bestowed upon him as a gift. In his absence that day, she observes the sequence of movements in her own body. She bends her knees, striving for the same ease, the assurance Régnier has in the flexibility of his limbs, she holds herself in the balance he manifests in that moment when everything is suspended. It could be his hands she sees, his fingers sweeping the earth as the other hand—with the independence of movement of a pianist or dancer—gropes for a container in her shoulder bag. She scrapes the arid soil with the edge of the jar, reproducing as best she can the jittery tension of the manoeuvre. She gets up and as she heads back to the building she tries to replicate his stride. It keeps her company in the vast landscape. Back in the silent lab, she puts on her safety gear and analyzes the sample.

It's almost too easy. In the most familiar place, on the ground she walks over every day, she finds it.

This is the moment at which Sadie understands that it is every-where. Alone in the lab, she recognizes it, the amphora beneath her microscope. She, too, has just opened a box, a movement rises in her, there it was, in the most familiar place, when they always travel so far, incredible, ridiculous distances when she thinks about it, when it turns out that every place is teeming with it, she has only to stretch out her arm, without the slightest effort. This sudden reversal of the calculation makes her dizzy, she can just bend over, wherever she is, and the virus is there. It's almost too easy, it suddenly seems indecent that it does not come at some greater cost, when life has shown her that you generally have to pay for anything vaguely resembling happiness. The new ubiquity of the virus uncovers a kind of splendour, an abundance to which, she thinks reflexively, she cannot be entitled.

Régnier will give her the honour of naming this one. She'll call it *Pandoravirus quercus*, for the oak.

She opens a file folder and takes out the orange notebook from her first seminar with Régnier. She kept it, and pulls it out from time to time, she likes flipping through it while she's thinking through a problem. Over the years, the time to which these notes belong has become more and more fragmented in her memory, and the substance of these written remnants has reacted upon contact with the successive discoveries made since. Her own intuitions are embedded in Régnier's questions and hypotheses, and by now she can no longer really distinguish between his thoughts and her own. Nevertheless, she has this strong feeling every time she opens the notebook: everything is already here.

She goes back over the pages covered in her scrawl, she rereads the sentences she left incomplete in her agitation. The meaning of some of her notes is completely garbled, and she tries to summon up what she had once been thinking. Her scribbles litter the pages like the corpses of tiny, misshapen creatures, as if they'd been crushed between the pages at random when she closed the book over two decades ago. These remnants sketch out the foundations of the new world that had upended everything she knew. Bits of Régnier's language carved their lines into a space that wasn't expecting them. But air has rushed in since then, continuing its corrosive work. When she looks back over this labyrinthine, discontinuous thread of language, it's not the words themselves that speak to her, but rather an inflection in the way they were inscribed on the page, the mark of a small catastrophe of perception, a line that skids off course, a mistake that disfigures language, all these tiny accidents that, portending the future, subtly disrupt the rigidity of the present, and hit her again with an echo of the blow to her mind that was this encounter with something that went beyond her ability to understand, and which still eludes her.

In the wild momentum of these notes, she also finds a trace of an erstwhile openness of her mind, something she struggles to name but which resembles a current that ran between Régnier's mind and her own, and allowed her to exist in a way that would otherwise have been inaccessible to her. Régnier is impossible, she's no longer looking for confirmation to that effect, but the impossibility of his life, which cannot accommodate his contours, has allowed for its extension into Sadie's life. Structuring Régnier's life allows Sadie in return to extend her own life beyond the limited space of her own mortal envelope.

Once again, in those first notes, she finds the notion of ubiquity that has just struck her at the foot of the oak tree, at that point not yet fully formed, still inarticulate under the cover of other questions and hypotheses, and it calls to her today in what she still holds of the unthinkable. In rereading these ideas, she finds a question, or a stream of questions, which have never been fully answered, scientific progress has supplied partial responses but has never truly sounded their depths.

As two threads of memory intersect accidentally, a tune comes back to her, a song she knew a long time ago. This is one of the risks of returning to these traces of the past—sometimes the current regurgitates some partially decomposed garbage. "J'ai planté un chêne," a song about a man who planted an oak at the edge of his field, a song by a great Québécois singer that her father liked to sing on Saturdays when he took her along to look at houses he fantasized about buying. A father and his daughter, chosen from among all the children to hold the wheel while he consulted maps through bleary eyes. It was her job to say "red, stop" or "okay, green, go," and he would work the pedals. Each week, her father would announce his dream of transplanting the whole family, of finding a new place where he was sure that the many elements sowing chaos in their life would be put in their rightful place once and for all. The other children were jealous of Sadie, they would also have liked to be part of the exclusive club of this elsewhere that was the subject of so much hopeful talk but that they never got a glimpse of. Her siblings would become vicious, they hated her, believing she had access to this place, that she was maybe even stealing a little bit of its sparkle while they were left with its cold ashes. It was true, after all, that their father loved Sadie more than the others. It was true that she was the one he brought along into his delusions. Their mother confirmed it, she would corroborate the suspicions of Sadie's brothers and sisters: that girl was not to be trusted. And yet, their father did not really know how to love. All that the privilege gave Sadie was the best spot when it came time for the beatings. She was traumatized by none of this—her father's excesses, her mother's indifference; it made her a realist. And now, when she sees how people who were loved by their parents turn out, she thinks she did manage to escape something there.

In the car, as they drove along the country roads, her father would sing along to the song with a patriotic glee that foretold a coming unity, a time of great harmony that would not fail to include the man and his land. Young Sadie would have loved to share in that happiness, but she didn't know what to do with her father's sudden expansiveness, his overflowing joy. She sat silently on the seat next to him, as if transfixed by his good mood, which was as unpredictable as it was impossible to contain. The end of their journey soon brought them to yet another hovel, where her father's delusional ambitions crumbled at the sight of rotting wood in the damp air.

Sadie hears the song's refrain again and again, as if it is determined to spoil her joy with the memory of a happiness that remained out of reach. And yet, this is something to celebrate, the discovery of a virus she is used to chasing around the world, the virus that drags her and all her gear over land and sea. This virus she now knows is actually close at hand all the time. She locks the lab and goes back outside, hoping the mistral will sweep out her memory, a wild wind to sweep everything clean.

XX

Régnier is lying on the bed next to her, editing an article while she puts the final touches on a grant application. One of Molly's playlists is playing over the speakers. Nancy Sinatra sings "How Does That Grab You, Darlin'?"

Sadie keeps an eye on him. All day long a subtle disturbance has been stirring in his system, just below the surface. She is waiting for him to decide to erupt. She doesn't press, but she doesn't lower her guard either. All day long she has been in a state of alert tension. "Could you turn it down, please." A demand, not a request. There they are. All day long, on edge. She knew the music would be too much. She gets up, lowers the volume, and then sits back down without jostling the bed. She knows that Molly's presence, through the music, bothers Régnier. He doesn't like it when signs of her other world make themselves known.

"My ears are *extremely* sensitive today," Régnier says, grimacing. His plastic face changes with his moods. She knows very well that he wants her to turn it off, but she lets the playlist switch over to a

Gainsbourg track, she knows it will annoy him, the bongos will bring them into a high-risk zone. She generally doesn't insist, in the lab in particular she doesn't allow herself any leeway, but sometimes she pushes back a little, she steps a little closer to the edge.

At her apartment, the sheets smell too strong, even though she buys unscented detergent. And on top of that it's noisy, her apartment overlooks Rue Bussy l'Indien, between La Plaine and the Cours Julien, where life unfolds at all hours beneath her windows. Sadie loves living in this tumult. She has immersed herself in it ever since she arrived in the city, she lets Marseille buzz around her, creates her own little bubble in all the commotion. When Régnier reminds her of the constant intrusions from the outside world—her apartment is a bit decrepit, the cracked walls don't keep out drafts or humidity, the neighbourhood is noisy—she shrugs. But beneath that nonchalance, she is proud to live below her means, she sees it as a sign of her independence. She likes the simplicity of feeling like she could live anywhere. Sometimes when she lies awake at night, the scent of spray paint rises up to her windows, and she falls back asleep to the low, comforting voice of the tagger.

"Can you turn off that lamp, it's unbearable at this hour." He is wrung out by the aggressive wattage. The lighting is never right. She keeps all the lights on and it drives him crazy. The old habits of a little Québécoise, from the land where electricity costs nothing. In Régnier's eyes, Sadie has never really fully adopted a French identity. He hears traces of her accent here and there, her tongue turning in unexpected ways. Most people don't pick up on it. She has adopted their manners and style, so they are fooled by her exterior, but Régnier can see the seams, and when her background seeps out through the cracks, it's a little shock to his ears. But it's true that this is also part of his attachment to her. He likes being the one who knows who she really is. He could never be this close with a French woman.

By the time Sadie met him, Régnier had already made something of his life. He was in a relationship at the time, with a girl he'd met as a student in undergrad. Madeleine was wonderful, she came from a good family, all his colleagues envied him, but he never managed to forget that she'd been witness to his painful ascent. She had come with him to Montreal, and the day before their return to Marseille, he told her he'd already rented a room and would be moving out as soon as they were back. When Sadie had agreed to follow him to France and work with him, he thought they would end up living together eventually. He liked the idea of continuity in his lifestyle. They would keep their relationship under the radar while she worked on her thesis, and then when the time came to make it public, she would go work at another university, preferably in another city. But things didn't quite work out that way. When this young woman, barely twenty, had showed up in his office, yes, he had recognized an astonishing, lively intelligence that managed, here and there, to pierce through the air of resignation that weighed her down. But her general tendency toward apathy had given him the false impression that she would easily adapt to the arrangements he had in mind. He had chalked up the spontaneous way she came to see him to American manners, which he did appreciate for the way they naively cut through academic hierarchy. It turned out that, while Sadie, in her radical self-sufficiency, didn't ask much of him either emotionally or practically, her tireless work ethic soon demanded everything of him.

Régnier loathes spending time at Sadie's place, in that shabby apartment where she lives as though she were just passing through. She notices none of the constant interruptions, the neighbours, the street, even the furniture at her place seems to cry out in distress. If he had only been able to do without her company, if he had managed to limit their contact to the controlled space of the lab, things would have been easier. But her presence, which he must admit made his life more or less bearable, was a whim he could not shake, to the point he had to admit that she had become a necessity.

It is, however, no easier to have Sadie stay at his place. Régnier is very protective of his space. He lives at Cité Radieuse, the modernist housing block designed by Le Corbusier. Every day, he enjoys the feeling of carrying out the most trivial tasks in a place designed by a genius, he has never grown indifferent to this elevation of daily hygiene. Charles-Édouard Jeanneret imagined this utopic housing project as the future of the working classes, and Régnier finds a particularly delicious irony in the fact that he has the means to live there only because he, the son of lowly farmers, deserted his social class. He liked living in a monument of History, until the department of tourism began organizing tours of the common areas. He plans to sell soon, he has been scouring ads looking for properties to buy, preferably something with a bit more privacy. Really, he was never made for the city. When he was younger, the feeling of urban aggression against his skin kept him in a state of productive tension. Sweating helped him think, and the overheated activity of the streets served as confirmation that enough distance separated him from the marshlands of his native Normandy. Now, even in the solitude of his insomnia, the city assails the walls of his Cité with an unending racket. He could always go settle down somewhere quiet, a country house near Aix-en-Provence, but it's not really his style, and it would also damage his rebellious image. There is a disgusted look he gets from Parisian academics when he says he lives in Marseille that he relishes too much to give up.

On the rare occasions Sadie stays at Régnier's, she can try all she likes to not move anything, to put the soap back in the same place in the bathroom, to not flood the soap dish, to not leave a single drop on the kitchen counter, to rearrange the cushions precisely, to recreate the correct sequence of folds in the lambswool blanket, she does her best to erase all traces of her passage through this space where every object has a designated and immutable place, but even just moving through the air in Régnier's apartment makes her acutely aware that she is disturbing a fundamental order. She never manages to recreate the harmony of which he alone knows the hermetic art. As if each object, and the encounter of each object with another object, were a system that was intuitive to him, something that existed inside him in the same way as his circulatory or digestive system. When she inevitably disrupts this system, she has the strong impression that she's hurting something inside him. When she takes a shower, he barges into the bathroom to beg her to turn off the water, she's wasting it, or can she sing less loudly, or what is that shampoo, he can smell it in the living room. She tolerates the intrusion, she knows he lives with all his nerves raw, exposed.

She tolerates it because, even after all these years, she can't help admiring what he creates, which depends on this mode of being. Everything that assails his senses also sharpens his intelligence. She tolerates it because he makes something of his madness—and not just by creating a sublime aesthetic. If Régnier can see what the rest of the world is blind to, if he's able to pull from the universal soup of existence an absolutely singular ordering that makes sense of the real, which strikes Sadie every time as the most important thing there is to think about, it's because the world is intimate to him. His unbridled narcissism makes him unbearable to other people, they cannot handle feeling their existence so nullified. Everyone except Sadie, who recognizes that this extension of self allows him to perceive the world with an almost superhuman acuity, as if its phenomena were striking his sensibility from the inside. Everyone except Sadie, who has room for the madness of others.

She deals with the frequent eruptions, she adapts, she made herself this way by assimilating the knowledge of his obsessions, their repetitions and their variations. She moves inside of his genius. She does not consider the different manifestations of his pathology as symptoms to treat, nor as phenomena that could be altered. She considers them the laws of this system of reality.

Régnier changed just once in his life. He climbed out of the ordinary, ancestral poverty he was born into, extricated himself from the drawer he had been filed away in by the French caste system. His success was a glitch in the social program. He had always stuck out, he was too intellectual, too sensitive, he didn't have a tough bone in his body, but he stayed the course, he hung on through the unpleasant years of adolescence thanks to his conviction that one day he would find a place where the extent of what he knew to be his formidable strengths would finally be revealed. During that time of patient waiting, he remained discreet and silent, cultivating an urge to fight that would serve him when the time came to break out of his rotten shell. His rise was successful. He corrected the errors of existence, he had wrested the means to do so from the universe, and he devoted the rest of his life to nurturing this advance on fate. Studying medicine was already quite a leap. The Régniers had not seen it coming, that their oldest son would become a professional. Focusing on research, on the other hand, was downright indecent. A researcher, and of viruses at that, the kid had really known how to piss them off.

XX

"Sadie, if you leave, it's going to be hell around here," her mother had said, closing the door on François Régnier, back when Sadie was preparing to leave.

When she saw Sadie arrive with him, she had realized there was a weak link in the chain. Stiffly but politely, Sadie's parents had invited Régnier to take a seat in the living room. Sadie had told them about her new plans, and Régnier had backed her up, making the case for her obvious talents, her brilliant future in research. There was a particularly cruel irony in it for her parents, who had done everything they could to get their eldest daughter to go into medicine like them. Her decision to study philosophy had already been an insult. Her father had fallen back on the hope that she would use it as the foundation of a political career, and when she had instead been drawn to metaphysical concerns, he worried but didn't stop trying to persuade her. Her mother, who was more of a realist, had already given up on the sly and stubborn daughter whose father loved her too much. But for all that, she would not easily loosen her grip on the idea of family unity. It was a matter of balance. Each member had their role to play, whether they liked it or not. A single defection would threaten the integrity of the whole.

Sadie's parents were doctors themselves. Her mother had been one of the only women in her class, following in the footsteps of her own father, a country doctor in Ontario. She met Sadie's father at medical school. How did an ardent Quebec nationalist fall in love with an Anglo girl from a Protestant family in Ontario? That was part of the mystery surrounding the beginnings of their relationship, about which Sadie knows very little. Her father was a short, proud man who never sat still, with an expressive face and jet black hair. Her mother was tall, thin, pale, and phlegmatic, impossible to impress. The more excited and overheated her father became, the more space he took up in the room, the more her mother withdrew behind a fortress of Victorian frigidity. This is not to say they were incompatible, necessarily; they fit together perfectly, but in a disastrous way. The excesses of one aligned perfectly with the deficiencies of the other, keeping them in a state of perpetual inflammation. In this caustic life, her father was never not flying off the handle, her mother frozen in an anesthesia of the senses. And yet, against any logic Sadie could muster after the fact, there had been a moment when they'd chosen each other.

Immediately after their wedding, they set out for Toronto, where Sadie's father would do his surgical residency. They were married at the end of April, and by the beginning of May, Sadie's mother was holed up at her parents' house in Oakville, in the Toronto suburbs. Nobody ever knew what was negotiated that summer within the walls of the house on Heritage Way, between the young Mrs. Dr. X and her parents, not even Sadie's father. But in September, without a word, her mother went back to the little rented apartment in the east end of Toronto and started her own residency. Sadie's father hated those years in Ontario, in a world of people who looked down on him and made it clear he didn't belong; even in the corridors of the hospital, the other doctors called him the frog. At the end of his program, they returned to Montreal together, and she dropped out of her pediatric residency to give birth to their first child, their daughter Sadie. This English name was, without question, the first thorn she planted in her husband's side. When a second child was born, her father rushed to announce he would be named François. Her mother named the third child Patrick. Her father said: Patrice. Next was Sadie's first sister, Marie. By the time Françoise was born, her mother had given up.

When she still lived in Montreal, Sadie often tried to imagine what might have become of her parents had they not gotten married. There must have been some other arrangement of destiny, in some parallel universe, a pathway to other lives in which they were better versions of themselves. As a child, before going to sleep, Sadie would pray hard that the night would find some way of separating them, cast the spell that would reshuffle the deck. Their life seemed to her an aberration. Sadie was ready to sacrifice herself to allow another story to unfold, even if it meant disappearing. Her own existence simply had to be the result of a mistake, she had to believe she was living in the wrong version. In the darkness of her bedroom, she watched as fragments of reality unfurled, clinging to the beams of headlights from outside and slipping away with them as they flashed by. In those furtive scenes, those portraits she barely retouched, the features of people she'd met out in the world mingled with those of her parents; she gave one the gentle disposition of a schoolteacher, the other the cheerful laughter of a passerby. But her theatre had to be recreated every night, and she never managed to arrive at its final form. The night and its infinite possibilities always ended up spitting her back out into the same absurd day.

It seemed, however, that she was the only one to notice the absurdity of the little dramatic production. Her parents were generous, altruistic people, driven by a deep commitment to social justice. Everyone who knew them agreed. When they first arrived in Montreal, they'd moved to a working-class neighbourhood in the city's east end, where they ran a clinic out of their home between their shifts at the hospital, treating people in the neighbourhood for free. For Sadie's father, this was a patriotic duty, and for her mother, an educational mission. They were redistributing the gifts life had given them. Even after they'd left the east end, her mother continued working with the very young and the very old, imparting her principles of health, hygiene, and education to the most vulnerable, and always leaving it to others to fall apart.

The members of this family were held together by the idea of some Goodness that transcended their individual existences, a Goodness that could absorb all the misfortune of daily life. In their east end neighbourhood, these class defectors were not just tolerated, but welcomed. The feeling of being needed kept a serene look on her mother's face, a sincere smile on her father's.

People they ran into on the street would crouch down to tell Sadie how lucky she was to have such good parents.

If you leave, it's going to be hell around here.

In the microscopic world, the extracellular matrix holds the knowledge of its own dispersion. Human collectives, even in their simplest expression, stubbornly resist this dispersion—which is the only thing that makes a future possible for the individual.

Sadie doesn't know where she acquired the knowledge of dispersion. When the microscopic life revealed it to her, years later, she understood that it had been acting all around her and she just hadn't recognized it. She hadn't recognized that everywhere around her, to an extent that far exceeded her own knowledge, the intelligence of separation and departure was already at work.

XX

A little more than five years after Sadie moved to France, her father, travelling with her youngest sister, Françoise, contacted Sadie for the first time. They had just landed in Paris and were planning to take the train south a week later. On the day of their arrival, she met them at their hotel on the port, and they went to eat seafood at Toinou.

He hadn't changed much, he was just a little gaunt, which accentuated the angles of his face. His hair and eyes were the same deep black. He did seem a bit shorter. Sadie's sister was also very small, and she bore a strong resemblance to their father. The same hair, the same dark eyes. She had that same restless look, a ferment of nerves visible on the surface. As the eldest sister, Sadie had tried to protect her siblings while she was still living at home. Françoise was barely ten years old when she left. Now she was fifteen. Sadie couldn't tell whether her sister remembered when she'd lived with them. She was nervous, visibly uncomfortable alone with their father in this entirely new place. Yet their father seemed relaxed, almost cheerful. He was exhilarated by the sea air, briskly cracking prawn shells and gulping down the flesh of the whelks with gusto.

Toward the end of the meal, their father got up to go to the bathroom, and Françoise rushed to tell Sadie, stretching out her neck level with the fish: "When I get back to Montreal, I'm going to live with Mom. She rented an apartment, in NDG, she already bought furniture, and she told me that when I get back, we're all going to go live with her, without Dad. But don't say anything to him because he doesn't know yet." Sadie, dumbstruck, couldn't detect any particular emotion in her teenage sister's face beyond relief at finally being able to unburden herself of this secret. When they said goodbye, Sadie embraced her sister, then her father. Marseille seemed to be doing him good.

She had already left all of that behind, and the next episode unfolded as if on a screen, in some inaccessible reality. So her mother had decided to save her own skin, and to take the remaining children with her. Sadie sometimes thinks back to that dinner, replaying the scene, searching among the soft bodies of the mollusks, the empty shells, for some sign that he might have known what awaited him back home.

XX

It's the end of the night at Scum. Veronica, Molly, and Sadie are chatting, passing a last joint back and forth. The bar is empty, the sun is nearly up. Being together makes it easier to watch the last of the night slip away. Molly puts on a track by the Crystals and dances around a little, limping. She can barely stand by now, thanks to a daring but meticulously calculated mix of amphetamines and alcohol, which remains her substance of choice as other trends come and go. For Molly, drugs are recreational, but her alcoholism is a matter of well-being, allowing her to come undone without leaving any evidence. She's busy proclaiming for the millionth time her love for the era of choirs, the golden age of entwined voices. She declares once again that the solo voice will soon take centre stage, toward the end of the millennium... Then she starts slurring her words, her story bogs down. "That's all a choir is for now... to bring out the virtuosity of one voice..." Sadie's heard this before. Soon, more and more female singers will record their own choirs, their voices reverberating to create the illusion of many. Molly doesn't stop, she has too much to say and is getting tangled up in shaky comparisons, she can't stop herself, but Sadie has never seen her totally lose her bearings. "The disappearance of the choir," Veronica concludes, struggling to keep her eyes open.

Sadie watches them fading despite their best efforts, she's getting foggy too, but her thoughts won't rest. The song in the background has its own intelligence. The knowledge of murmurations of birds, a knowledge that revolves around harmony, and listening. The viruses have that voice too, Sadie thinks, her mind still working even at the very end of the night. The voice of the choir. In the world of the virus, the walk to the front of the stage means nothing. The effort to keep herself from drifting off almost hurts. The virus does not advance . . . strictly speaking, its movement . . . has nothing to do with our sense of direction. She imagines that the life of the virus, which circulates by other means than natural selection, invents another way of moving through time. Her eyes focus as best they can while her mind reaches for images, but next to her, the two girls are quickly unravelling. The virus doesn't need the relatively exceptional event of the meeting of two gonads to make its way in the world. It has time to spare. It can go to sleep in the permafrost and wake up millions of years later without a wrinkle. Molly is lolling in the leatherette booth, her limbs liquid, while Veronica floats, her eyes half open onto the void. The virus is free of the constant weight, the growing weight of years, that each day presses the body a little further up against the limits of the finite life. Molly and Veronica are no longer as beautiful in these last hours of the night, these women who are usually so magnificent, almost too beautiful, it almost hurts Sadie, they don't know when to stop and so the work of art they make of themselves ends up saturated, gorged to the point of obstruction, in these last hours it's like standing before a painting so thick with paint you can no longer see anything. That's what it is, too much paint, a thick and stodgy layer.

X X

One beautiful Sunday afternoon in April, Sadie is having a few drinks at a bar near La Plaine when her phone rings, a private number. Her father's voice sobers her up instantly. One of his colleagues at the hospital heard about the Pandoravirus that Sadie's team isolated in a Berlin eyeball, and she thinks she might have found something similar in a Montreal leg. Her father is calling, after years of silence, to offer her a virus. His love language.

Like the time he operated on Molly's sister, Ida, who was living in Montreal and had a brain tumour the size of a grapefruit. It cost Sadie something to call him, but for Molly, she would have done much worse. When Ida came to visit, a year into full remission, she kept saying, over and over, in her Swedish-inflected French: "Sadie, your father is a saint, he's a saint! Un saint, Sadie!" She pronounced the T at the end of the word, having never heard it said aloud in French before. Sadie restrained herself from telling Ida that he had removed her cancer to inoculate her with an even more vicious agent. She held back because Ida had been through a lot and needed to hold onto her belief that there was goodness in this world, which had become alien to her from the inside, in that glacial city—even for someone who'd grown up in Stockholm—where she'd spent the winter alone in her badly heated apartment, too weak to drag her radiation-ravaged carcass out into the icy streets, she'd even had to ask friends to take in her pit bull, Marianne, she couldn't manage the walks anymore. Molly's sister had been very alone, except for the tumour doing an excellent job eating away at her brain. Sadie felt responsible for the fate of this girl, knowing she was trapped in a Montreal winter when Sadie had escaped it. She called up Dr. X, who was surprised to hear from her after years of silence but pleased that she was asking him for something. He got excited and carried away on the phone, it was as if they had spoken just the day before, as if they were old colleagues, he was always ready to make himself useful of course, he jumped at the opportunity to show her a side of himself that she might simply have missed all these years.

She can't deny that he's an artist with the scalpel. Ida showed her the scar, she parted the nest of golden curls that had grown back strangely quickly and with a luxuriance that seemed to celebrate her triumph over the disease, another miracle of the sainted doctor no doubt, and she revealed the line in her flesh as if it were a secret pathway.

"Sadie, you don't understand, he's the best! It's gone, it's completely gone!" She grabbed Sadie's finger with an energy surprising for her still-emaciated body, and placed it on what you could barely call a scar, it was so fine and smooth, a fold that wanted so badly to disappear that it was barely perceptible to the touch. A mark striving for its own erasure, this was what made her father's reputation, what set him apart from his colleagues. The art of his sutures.

It has almost disappeared by now, it's only visible up close, very close to Sadie's forehead, just beneath her hairline. Even then you'd have to know what you're looking at, a subtle discolouration. A summer day. Summer vacation was always hard. Their father loved to take them on the road, but organizing everything required a lot of him, there were guidelines to follow, very precise rules that would ensure that everything fit in the car on the strict condition that they were respected with the utmost rigour. Putting disparate elements in order was another of Dr. X's specialities. Everything was planned down to the centimetre, so that all of life itself would fit precisely into the space available in the family-sized vehicle. But inevitably, some element proved resistant to this operation. That day, it was Sadie. Never again, after that. You don't learn anything, really, unless you learn it with your body. Another piece of fatherly wisdom. Only the body's memory really integrates knowledge, and her father is one to know what the body knows. The frontal bone is incredibly resilient, which makes it the ideal place to instill an education, particularly in what you might call the most insolent of minds. The temples are off limits, too soft. Sadie had the biggest forehead of all her siblings, she was the most hard-headed, her father said. Things got muddled quickly, her father did not appreciate stubbornness, he struck the child right in her big, hard forehead. After the shock of the spurting blood that gave a minor injury the appearance of a massacre, everyone was brought inside to suture, with implacable logic, the rupture the incident had caused in the order of things. Her father stitched in the kitchen while her mother lectured the stunned children. She passed on the good news, in case they had missed it in the course of the day's events—their father's discipline always served to bring them a little closer to Goodness.

Once they were on the road, with the fabric of the family mended, everything was different. Her father's mood brightened instantly. He was never one to let anger fester, always quick to wipe the slate clean after a fuss. He loved to see the countryside. He would sing heartily, and the children would eventually fall asleep, squeezed in on top of each other, their damp thighs and clammy arms sticking together to create a single sleeping mass drenched in sweat. The mass was shaken awake at every village they passed through, from one end of Quebec to the other, so that the children could wave at all the locals sitting on their front porches. Their father would say that it was better to wave at ten people you didn't know than to risk not greeting one you did. During those weeks that the family traversed the province from campsite to campsite, the comforts of home were never far. Their mother made veal cutlets on the camp stove, because camping was no reason to not eat as well as they did at home, as their father used to say. Each member of the family had a role to play in the logic of the trip, and it was incumbent upon each of them, above all, to enjoy the adventure, and adventure, as he liked to say, in his best Jacques Brel imitation, begins when your hands are washed by the light of dawn. The most important thing is to never just be along for the ride.

He loved these parentheses in time that protected this little world from its usual constant scattering. Nobody was immune to temporary mood swings, but generally speaking, their father maintained a pleasant enough disposition during those nomadic journeys, which gave him the time and space to bend the hours of the day to his personal precepts, to the many maxims that expressed his principles for a healthy life.

A saint, Sadie.

X

She's startled, she'll think about it, she says. A virus as an offering. He's giving her the opportunity to atone with this oblation for the crime of her defection—because it is this estrangement she must sacrifice on the altar of science. He wants to see her put on the lab coat, pull on the gloves, he wants them to don the ceremonial attire together. He knows that she'll respond to the virus. He knows that she'll get on a plane, he knows how easy it is for her. Her suitcase so light, the bare minimum, everything fits effort-lessly, all the necessities packed up with ease. He knows nothing of her life anymore. But he knows she's prepared to answer when the virus calls.

XX

"No, it's not dangerous." People are often reflexively wary when Sadie tells them what she does for a living. She has to reassure them, give them details on the precautions they take daily, and as the conversation unwisely continues and more information emerges—"wait, did you say giant viruses?"—she has to provide reassurances—"and…why exactly do you wake these viruses up?"—and offer guarantees. Their eyes open wide each time, it's a reflex, and then they keep an eye on her, sidelong glances, as if she were a child playing in her parents' medicine cabinet, or, more often as she gets older, an old biddy off to run down some pedestrians with her car.

At first, she thought it would reassure people a little if she made it clear from the outset that she studies viruses that have no direct interactions with humans, which is to say, that are not pathogenic to our species. Yet this assurance generally makes people just as suspicious, but in a different way, that is not as easy to clearly articulate. They should be relieved, but are somehow even more troubled. Even within the scientific community, people are primarily interested in viruses in the context of their parasitic relationships with us, human beings, as agents of infection. The fact that Sadie was not interested in viruses from a perspective in which the human being is the host, but rather studied them as something that would cohabitate with us without being overly concerned with our existence—that bothered people.

This doesn't mean that we don't interact with them at all. But she is generally careful not to bring that part up.

X

Berlin. An inflamed eyeball, at the Charité-Universitätsmedizin. When the white of the eye loses its transparency, a whole network of aggressive little red veins appears. The patient goes to the hospital on the advice of his doctor, who suspects his conjunctivitis is getting worse. At the Charité, the doctors perform the routine tests. The patient wears contact lenses, they send those to the lab, they ask him to bring in his contact case, and they send a sample from that to the lab too. Their goal is to isolate, according to protocol, whatever is causing the inflammation of the cornea. The specialist already knows what he'll find, a simple amoeba called *Acanthamoeba*, often found in soil or fresh water, a micro-organism that mostly goes about its business without bothering anyone, but that sometimes turns predatory and infects an animal or even a human. So the doctor sends off the samples to the lab like any other ordinary test and waits for the results without much apprehension. But once the samples arrive at the lab, they will take on an unexpected and unforeseen value, and will disrupt—at first minimally, and then more and more significantly—the transactional nature of the relationship between the doctor and his patient with the inflamed eye. Were it not for the somewhat over-zealous work of a lab technician at the Charité hospital in Berlin, the uneventful identification of the microscopic culprit would have been the end of the story. A few antibiotics and off you go. But it turns out that, in this case, the infectious bacterium is itself infected by what will be identified in the days that follow as a new branch of the *Pandoraviridae*. *Pandoravirus inopinatum*, for the element of surprise.

Knowing what lives on contact lenses, Sadie could never wear them. Those tiny extensions of the body often become home to a fascinating assortment of micro-organisms. Attaching themselves to the surface of the lens, these micro-organisms form a consor-tium, the bacteria clumping together to produce a sticky network, a matrix that provides a protective and supportive environment for the cells that proliferate there. The majority of observers would look at this assembly and see nothing more than a slimy membrane formed by chance, but to the initiated eye, it's a verit-able community organization created by the micro-organisms and, unlike our sprawling cities, it's a system that the citizens can adapt to changes in the environment.

The life of these agglomerations, these microbial cities, does have a cyclical rhythm, however: once it reaches an advanced stage of maturity, the city disperses. For its citizens to survive, they must learn the art of separation. The matrix possesses the agents of its own destruction, and periodically sends the bacteria and other micro-organisms off to continue their life elsewhere, armed with what they have learned from their forced co-operation in a densely populated environment.

[BIS REPETITA]

When she opens her eyes, her head against the airplane window, it's impossible to tell how far the immense metal shell has come in its journey. Sadie has lost track of time, she overdid it a little on the pills before boarding the plane. Now she emerges, within these steel entrails, gripped by anxiety. The milky light blinds her, she'd wanted to dull the experience of return, but now her senses are betraying her, the white water is at her throat, seaweed tangled up in the window and wrapping itself around her head. She does know that it's impossible, she knows where she is and where she's going, but her senses deceive her and recognize the sensation of the crossing, a moment suspended in time.

This is why she went by boat the first time she crossed this ocean, to have more of that suspended time. She'd read an article about soldiers in the Gulf War who were taken home by plane, their nervous systems giving out under the shock of the contrast, the overlap of irreconcilable realities.

She doesn't know what she's looking at, and then her eyes adjust painfully to the view, the whiteness takes on a cottony texture, she places herself here, somewhere in the clouds of an unidentified sky. It could be the sky over Greenland. Or Labrador. Because they are heading west, that much she knows. They are moving backward in time, in an interminable sunset. She looks at the book closed on her lap, her finger still marking her page. Usually, she spends most of a flight reading, but this time she can't focus, her vision is blurred, nothing can overcome the nausea, the hallucination (but she does know this is impossible!) that the plane is bringing her back in the opposite direction of the transatlantic crossing she made twenty-five years ago. As if she were sitting in one of those train seats facing against the direction of travel, her head spins, her heart is liquid. She closes her eyes again somewhere over Iceland, or Greenland, or Newfoundland. In her mind, she goes even further. In the red flesh of her eyelids, she sees herself flying over the Great Lakes, then the Prairies, continuing on with the sun toward the snowy mountains of British Columbia...

X

Sadie wakes up without managing to fully resurface. Her mouth is fuzzy. She tries to swallow to moisten her throat, but her tongue is scratchy and dry. She looks at her watch, straining her eyes, and tries to calculate the time difference, the hours that have passed and the hours left to go, she should be there by now, yes, a few hours more at most, almost no time at all and she'll be there. She tries to check on the map projected on the little screen in front of her—no, she's not there yet. She reaches for clarity, tries to locate herself in a present moment that is losing its consistency, but like in a dream, everything gets tangled up. In this abyss in the middle of the sea, she reaches out but touches nothing.

She can't turn back now. Europe suddenly seems to her an intangible idea. She clings to the project that must carry her through. She turns herself in its direction, she tries to make its outlines appear in her mind. But ahead, the past stares back at her from empty eye sockets. No, she tries again. Ahead, the virus is active, busy; ahead, the surprises that may await. She has to, yes that's it, she has to look ahead. She's almost there—but her head can't keep up.

Suspended between two worlds, she tries to stare at a point in the distance, as she learned to do for motion sickness. But there's nothing out there but white, woolly white, milky white, everywhere. She tries to find clarity, to dissipate this thick atmosphere of nothingness around her—she's almost there, she'll be there soon.

She returns, during this flight, to her previous transatlantic crossing. The voyage in the other direction had stretched on without end, days and nights. And at night, her father's voice began to sound in the submerged hull, in the corridors of the ship, his cries drowning in the eddies of the sea, her wounded father, she heard his lament day and night, it seemed, the length of an interminable night, the long crossing allowed it, created a space for her pain, an anguish irrigating the arteries of the massive steel fish that would carry her to her future.

A hand on her shoulder pulls her sharply back to the present, the flight attendant hands her a plastic cup so she can pour her a little water. Sadie tries to collect herself, she takes the cup, it all feels far away, very far, by repeating this it will come true. But like the clouds, like the sky outside, like the still-invisible Earth, she can't quite make out where it begins and where it ends.

PART 2

MONTREALIS

XX

As far back as she can remember, Sadie's parents often hosted visitors from out of town and held dinners in their honour. Most often they were other physicians, from Europe, Latin America, Africa. This is no different, she thinks, as the taxi skirts the mountain on Côte-Sainte-Catherine, heading from Côte-des-Neiges toward the colossal English-style mansions perched on the side of the mountain that signal the entrance to the chic neighbourhood of Outremont, for those who might not have already grasped the shift in social status. Her parents bought the house on Querbes when she was twelve, and that was when she came to understand that she was part of the bourgeoisie, and not the working classes among whom she'd spent her childhood. Nobody explained it to her, but she noticed that the kids in her new neighbourhood behaved differently, and that there were far more parks and trees here than in her east end neighbourhood. For a long time, she thought her mother had been behind the move, that was the excuse her father gestured at without ever making it explicit to each guest, not wanting to be lumped in with the neighbourhood snobs. During their first meal in the new house, her father sat in silence for a long moment, looking around the vast dining room, and then announced that they would never be happy in this place. Nevertheless, he stayed, long after her mother had left to live on Harvard, west of the mountain.

From the taxi, she sees a few ultra-Orthodox Jewish families walking down the sidewalk. She spent her teenage years living next door to Hasidic families and has not encountered that community in France. She used to enjoy running into those clusters of silent people who would never look at her, except the children, who played like any other kids except that they shouted and laughed in Yiddish. She liked experiencing their indifference to her life, unlike her father, who was offended by it. To him, these neighbours seemed to want to remind him that he was not at home there. And yet, this was precisely why he'd avoided the Anglophone neighbourhoods, why he refused every invitation from his wife's aunt in Westmount. Outremont was already complicated for him. The only reason they could afford the house on Querbes was because the prospect of Quebec independence had led to the flight of the Anglo-Canadian upper classes, and the void created by this exodus sucked in a Francophone population who would otherwise have been unable to access such prestige. Dr. X was ashamed of rushing toward this newly deserted empire along with his neighbours. He didn't say it in so many words, but Sadie could see it in the way he defended himself to foreign visitors, explaining the dynamics of the city. He was ashamed to be part of a small Francophone elite who dreamed only of shopping at Ogilvy and were proud to say they taught at the Université francophone de la Montagne, adding for the benefit of those from elsewhere: the French McGill. In the Quebec that was his country, people knew where they came from and they didn't genuflect before the divinities of English, or worse, American money. But the indifference of the Hasidim was painful to him in another way. He was accustomed to being scorned for his specific identity, and that kind of threat stimulated his pride. But the Hasidim's disregard didn't directly address him in any individual way; in fact, it erased his singularity. He didn't know how to respond to it. Sadie, in contrast, was fascinated by their detachment. She saw it as the outer facade of an exclusive ecstasy, jealously guarded within hermetic walls, except for the murmur that escaped in the evening from the frosted windows of the synagogues on Hutchison or Bernard. As a teenager, she'd go for walks alone and slow down to hear their singing, grazing the walls of the synagogues just to get close to the joy from which she was excluded.

X

She returns as a stranger. She's just passing through, she tells herself again and again to block out the voices on the radio, the local news she wants none of, she's only visiting, yes, she's here on business, as she told the customs agent, the taxi driver, she's here to pick up her virus and then leave, she's holding her breath for the duration of a dive and then emerging from the icy waters, it's April and the ice is starting to melt, it was forming a moving checkerboard on the Saint Lawrence as the plane began its descent, a particularly dangerous time of year for anyone who gets the idea to venture out onto the ice, the surface may seem solid enough but one step too far and you're drowning in what remains bright and bracing just beneath it.

So don't stop too long, distribute your weight equally, step by step, until you reach solid ground. Now that she has crossed the Atlantic frozen by time, she'll barely set foot on the other side before leaving again. Always beware of the thaw. It's not in her to be wary, however; fear is not a scientific attitude. She constructs hypotheses, yes, but mostly she bases her ideas on fact. The spring thaw is the best time of year for pathogens, that is a fact, she's here for a reason. There's an insouciance in the spring air that Sadie has always found nauseating. As if everything could begin again from zero, as if the melting snow doesn't always just give us back the same old trash. Last year's dog shit doesn't get her quite as excited as it does these poor bastards in cold countries, sick of overheating in their stuffy shacks and thrilled to finally get outside and blow off some steam. For Sadie, who wakes up million-year-old viruses from permafrost, who has seen everything that time can collect and keep intact, there's not much in the thaw to rejoice about.

She lives far away from these seasons now, far from this cycle of radical transformation, the aggressive shift from icy winds to tropical heat waves. The people who live through the transition develop an exaggerated romanticism for its only vaguely bearable moments, the few weeks a year when their system isn't in a state of total shock, when their existence isn't reduced to brutal, animal survival. During those miraculous lulls, their imagination rushes to reinhabit their reclaimed humanity, going crazy over each new bud that emerges, each clod of earth uncovered, shucking off their swollen skin in the furious worship of renewal.

Gazing at the piles of dirty snow from which last fall's garbage is beginning to surface, almost intact, Sadie thinks to herself that nature might renew itself, but the human seasons just move around the same muck that will never decompose.

Her father's little joke to have her come at Easter. He's hidden a gift for her at the hospital, come on, let's do an Easter egg hunt, like when she was a child and he made them give away the few treats they got from their grandparents to the neighbourhood kids. Fine for those kids to eat junk. This time, Sadie will be able to keep her Easter virus. Come celebrate spring, we'll observe Lent if we have to, come on Sadie, just in time for the resurrection of the dead.

Just hold up a minute, Sadie, I hid a beautiful white rabbit in a leg half-eaten by an army of bacteria, just for you, you'll see, it's magnificent, a land of microscopic wonders. Come on, Sadie, let's finally celebrate a new beginning.

X

As the car moves along the small roads of their affluent neighbourhood, Sadie tries to visualize her father, all alone in his house. She has never known him outside of his marriage to her mother. There was that afternoon in Marseille, the seafood at Toinou, but what kind of process has been set in motion in him since she left home? He will have aged, of course. He is now seventy-six, seventy-seven years old. How did the loss of her mother's presence affect the evolution of his character? And how did it affect the corrosion of his being, a process that was already underway? He was in his fifties when her mother left, the last time Sadie saw him. What is that age like, anyway, those years between fifty and eighty? She's nearly there herself. Her father, at that age, found himself alone for the first time. She has so often imagined this separation, but left too soon to see what their lives were like once they were unencumbered by one another. Picturing this reality, when she's nearly there, at his house, is as difficult for her as it would be to believe that nature had suddenly reinvented a fundamental dynamic of living beings. For her, they were two inextricable systems of a particularly virulent symbiotic complex.

And yet, what Sadie sees upon entering the house is not a new specimen, a father stripped of his interaction with the mother. He opens the door, and as she takes her first step inside, she barely has time to take in the sight of this new old man before she notices her mother, sitting in the living room.

She has returned, she's home. Her mother turns her gaze on her, and Sadie sees something in her eyes she has never seen before. It's not age; she has changed little, on the whole. Her skin is smooth, her hair soft and styled, even if the impeccable waves have lost a little volume. Sadie recognizes the same composure in her manner, her posture. But the slightly unfocused look she gives Sadie is the kind one would give a stranger, an invited guest. There is a kindness in her mother's face, a sweet and unbearable benevolence. Against all expectations, reality has aligned with Sadie's fantasy, she is cloaked in strangeness, a hermetic protection that would allow her to be plunged back into this world and yet remain untouched by it. So this is what they saw, the visitors who came through the door all those years. A pleasant, affable woman.

Sadie's father goes upstairs to put her mother to bed. He comes back down a few minutes later and joins her in the kitchen. Sadie is sitting at one of the two spots where the round table is not covered in a heap of papers, newspapers, and documents of all kinds, stacked in dangerously teetering piles. He says that he has cut down his hours at the hospital. Sadie wonders if what was once called his exceptional rigour is less tolerated by the nurses now, and less confined to the medical protocol that made his reputation. Right now, standing in the middle of his cluttered kitchen, he looks like a man buried by time.

Her father makes coffee, launches into an explanation, effortlessly finding the appropriate expressions in a language whose accuracy covers a sufficient scope of reality, without risking going too much into depth. He sticks strictly to the medical vocabulary he's used to employing, he wields the terms designed for this type of situation with neutrality. The language comes easily to him, it does not sully his mouth, his tongue, he speaks with authority, not mincing words, he is not affected in the least by this language. He gives his interlocutor nothing to hold onto but strict turns of phrase, unequivocal articulations. It was designed this way. This language is intended to leave no margin of error.

Sadie, who has still not moved from her chair, is left with the dirty job of interpreting this for herself: her mother is senile. They are still married, so he took her home. Nobody said a word. Her mother left, then came home twenty years later another woman. Perhaps he finally has the wife he wanted. Sadie's head is spinning still from the pills she took on the plane. She's dizzy, her vagus nerve is taking the hit. Life will have found the key at last, the winning formula to reconcile the crazy woman and the old man. He didn't use words like crazy, Sadie's the one with the foul mouth.

Her mother has returned home a stranger. A young bride lagging a little behind. Her dress has been damaged in the meantime—it took her a while to find her way back, locate the address—the street has worn away at its hem. She has regained the look Sadie had seen in old photos. A look from before, from before the beginning. Her mother went back to Oakville, discovered another door through which she could emerge back into reality, into another life where she is reunited with her husband, where he will take care of her this time. No kids around, no shifts at the hospital, she is responsible for nobody now and all her time is her own. She experiences a new detachment, she smiles at the future. Her mother is dying of this new life, dying of the good life, at last.

Sadie's father expects a reaction. A few tears, maybe. He doesn't know who she is right now either. He doesn't know Sadie at this age, the age his wife was when she left him. He doesn't look at her, but Sadie can sense that he's waiting for her to wrap up his performance, his professional act. He's waiting for her to say something so he can get to the conclusion. She says: "When are we going to the hospital?"

X X

There is no knowledge that precedes the virus. It is the virus that, in its singularity, teaches us how to know it. Each new virus teaches Sadie how to study it.

The woman who welcomes father and daughter at the microbiology department security desk doesn't hide her excitement. They're almost there. She's the one who made the connection and alerted Dr. X. She knows Sadie's work. She introduces herself: Claire Jean-Baptiste. She manages the sequencing libraries for the genomic centre at the Hôtel-Dieu. Sadie's guts are a mess, she's struggling to focus. She watches herself, as if from a distance of a few inches, following the woman, Claire, who seems upon first glance like a cross between a gamer geek and an intractable librarian.

Finally bent over a microscope—her nervous system calms, her jaw relaxes little by little—she could almost forget that her father is right there. She immediately recognizes the formation, the amphorae stuck together. Sadie had asked them for a totally out-dated optical microscope, they couldn't believe it at the hospital laboratory. For a virus and for most bacteria, they usually got out the heavy artillery. Their cutting-edge technological vision allowed them to see nothing, their eyes fixed on the internal structures of these minuscule giants. They would have to change the dimensions, move back a little. It was when they took a step back that it would appear. A proliferation of amphorae.

Pandoravirus inopinatum. Like the one found by accident in Berlin. So this is what brought her back here. By accident. It's not interested in the human, but in the bacteria that attacks the human. What the bacteria chooses as a host is none of the virus's concern. As long as there's something to infect, it's happy, it makes do. The presence of the virus here, in a human wound, is pure coincidence. It remains a stranger to the hospitality of human flesh. It is entirely unaware of the fact that the man in whose leg the virus was found has had a brush with death. Even if it had gone that far, the virus would have kept doing what it was doing. The man is an important man, Sadie's father informs her. He knows him from the Party. A power broker, an influential figure. Illustrious flesh makes no difference to the virus, it's the bacteria that bore the brunt of it, for having dared to picnic in the wrong wound. In a less eminent leg, it would have prospered, but for such distinguished flesh, no treatment was spared. The bacteria had no chance. But the antibiotics don't touch the virus, which stays put, cozy in its petri dish.

Usually, Sadie would just take the virus and run. The work that follows will be arduous and delicate. This is bioinformatics now. Sequencing the virus's DNA, the most complex part of the work, will be done on-site at the lab in Marseille. In the tiny part of the virus we can perceive, nature is broken down even further into a multitude of genes to be analyzed and matched up in order to rewrite the equation of the code.

Deciphering the code will take several readings, a dive into the world of deep sequencing, the most advanced kind of genetic reading. Going deeper and deeper into the details of the world, that process produces more and more libraries of sequences at an incredibly high speed. All those layers of interpretation to put the code in order, to isolate something like a fingerprint, the signature of a creature that knows nothing of that business of reading.

Usually, Sadie calls Régnier immediately, day or night. Within minutes of encountering the giant and correctly identifying it, she calls Régnier, she gets on the plane again right away, by the next day at the latest she's on her way with the virus in hand. She arrives the following day, flights from North America to Europe are overnights. She returns to her home time zone, eliminates the distance that separates her from the lab and from Régnier. He's there, the day after at the latest, usually, in the morning, at the Marseille-Marignane Airport, he waits for her at the little café just outside the security zone, this costs him something, he would prefer to wait in the car, but he wants to show his appreciation, he knows how to make the right gesture when it counts, Régnier is no ingrate. The café is where she expects to find him. When the doors to the section reserved for travellers open before her, she is struck by the Mediterranean air. Each time she comes back from a trip, even just from Paris, it hits her, the power of that air that smells like pine. When he sees them coming, Sadie and her virus, he smiles. He opens his arms to her. Régnier is a grateful person.

Her absence has been felt in his daily life. He will now be shielded once again from many little disruptions. He welcomes her back into his intimate life.

There is no reason things shouldn't unfold that way.

XX

The car heads back north on Avenue du Parc. "Park Avenue,"
Sadie's mother would always say it in English. To infuriate her
father. To conjure up another city through these two words, *Park
Avenue*, the dream of another city, the vision of a Montreal of the
nineteenth century that would have been sister to the other great
North American city, New York. An island city like Manhattan,
breathing through the big park at its centre. The city had invited
the architect of Central Park, Frederick Law Olmsted, to design
the park on Mount Royal. Olmsted had great ambitions for
Mount Royal Park, a strategic abundance of vegetation that would
exaggerate the height of the mountain. The key was to focus on
green, Olmsted thought, to fend off the city that wanted to
encroach on the mountain. In the meantime, Montreal wound up
on the verge of bankruptcy, and in the 1870s, the city abandoned
Olmsted's plans in order to develop the park in a more econom-
ical way. In the park that Sadie knew, nothing had been kept of
the vegetation plan imagined by the illustrious American architect. Her mother sometimes took her slew of children on a stroll
down the length of Park Avenue, summoning up a little of the

grandeur Montreal had long since renounced. These walks with her children were one of the only pleasures she allowed herself, a sharp contrast to her daily regimen and her way of retaliating against the Francophone-Québécois worldview that circumscribed their lives.

Sadie's father would happily have stayed in Quebec City, near the lowlands of the Saint Lawrence, where his family had left its mark, generation after generation of prominent citizens. In the predigital age, to be a notary was to serve as Google for the entire village. There was great pressure on her father to take up the profession, or at least to go into politics. Becoming a physician was the extent of his rebellion. Sadie's mother would not entertain the idea of Quebec City. She hadn't left the suburbs of Toronto just to be cut off from the world in an average city of small business owners, where she would forever have been "l'Anglaise" to the petite bourgeoisie who had never been anywhere else, but didn't let that diminish their certainty that there was nowhere better. She acquiesced to Montreal; Sadie's father never took to it. He negotiated to raise their children in Francophone neighbourhoods only, those sections of the city where it was at least still possible to pretend that other city didn't exist in the shadows of his own, the other city where the country was always slipping further from the hands of French Canadians.

Sadie is back, she realizes it as she climbs back up the avenue that spans the whole island, south to north. She doesn't say a word, her jaw locked, the coat she brought isn't warm enough, she can see her hunched reflection in the car window, her frozen body curling in on itself. It's impossible to get lost in Montreal, in this grid, the city criss-crossed with never-ending streets. There are, of course, a few hiccups in the major thoroughfares, sometimes a road suddenly disappears only to reappear, offset, a little further on. But once you get your bearings, once you know where north is, the city has no further secrets, and it's impossible to hide. Every aspect of the city obeys a grid, language follows it, and so does culture, and so does social class. At least, that's how Montrealers conceive of the city, Sadie thinks. As you follow one of the major streets, north to south or east to west, you can see the different squares of the checkerboard, clearly divided. That hasn't changed. At the airport, the metro map surprised her with its simplicity. She'd expected it to have grown more complex since she left, but it had only extended its main lines into the suburbs. Montrealers are still prevented from moving about the city in any kind of anarchic fashion, any risk they might lose their sense of the grid is precluded. When people in France find out that Sadie grew up in Montreal, a fact she never divulges herself, they often bring up the underground city that stretches out mysteriously beneath its surface. That vision of Montreal's arteries alive with the alternate reality of the underground, the fantasy of a rebellious North America resisting the logic of major European centres, comes from people who have never set foot on the continent. It's true that it would have been quite natural to imagine other routes beneath an often-hostile surface, galleries of artificial life where bright lights would help cultivate a dense forest all year long, where people could move freely in intricate, flower-filled tunnels with no regard for the compartments of the city above. But to do that, to invent a different kind of city designed for the people that live in it, would take the kind of creativity and audacity that, as Sadie has been saying for years, is utterly lacking in Quebec's metropolis.

Here she is, again. As her defensive state continues, a dull numbness overtakes her, threatens to encyst her limbs, her mind. She had practically forgotten that numbness. She reprogrammed her body in the intervening years, she no longer lives inside a shell. Sadie's father is bringing her home. Father, mother, daughter, together again under the same roof.

But she saw it, her virus is definitely here. She clings to this fact, which allows her to shake off reality. The virus is the reason for her presence here, the virus is what brought her back. The fluke hospitality of a bacterium that brought the virus into the human world. As for the tragedy weighing her down because of that human world, the virus is barely aware of it. Sadie reassures herself that, despite her current circumstances, she's still the one who leaves, that's who she is in the world, that's the direction of her life. Onward, into the distance. Far from the domestic bullshit, far from the ridiculous familial refrain echoed by the eternal chorus of Montreal, of Quebec, of America's amnesia. She prefers her bullshit with the flavours of elsewhere. France babbles too, but Sadie doesn't recognize herself in its refrain. Marseille is crazy, but it's a craziness she can love. She always stands slightly apart, a refugee from the echolalia of familial vows. Thou shalt not leave... *Or it's going to be hell around here.*

Her unknown virus, her great unexpected discovery, bursts in to summon her again, this time to the hell of that same old refrain.

It's not the first time the virus has pulled this old trick of popping up in the most familiar places. Sadie recognized its ubiquity at the foot of the oak tree just steps from the lab. It was with *Pandoravirus quercus* that it became clear—this was not just the story of an ancestor lost in the sediment of time. An antiquity that had forgotten to disappear. An anachronistic anomaly. It was as if the extraordinary trips to the ends of the earth, on distant seas, had allowed researchers to believe in an exceptional rarity, when in fact it was right there, everywhere, beneath their feet, and maybe even in the cells of their own body. A very important man, Sadie's father had said, softly, referring to the infected man from whom the virus had been taken. He, too, wants to believe in an exception, a kind of chosen one. But we know now that the presence of this virus in the world is neither exception nor aberration. It's trying to tell us something we don't yet know how to decode. These are not solitary vestiges of a bygone era, but entire families of giant viruses, surrounding us. These tiny giants are everywhere. The secret's out. But we cannot yet read this multitude. We only see it by chance, and human beings are not very good at coping with chance.

The car skirts Mount Royal on the way up to Outremont. The whole way back, Sadie doesn't say a word, she replays the film of the microscope for herself, to bring movement back into the feeling of inertia. She replays the appearance of elliptical formations, their work of inhabitation. She replays, again and again, the visible movement, she holds on tight to the precious idea: the virus is not the box through which it appears to us, the virus is not its particle, not its membrane, the virus is not the exterior shell, it is not the visible. The virus is that which comes to life inside the life it infects. When she holds onto it, when she clings fiercely to these convolutions of negation, the sinuous folds around the indefinable life of the virus, the idea brings her back to movement.

X

Back at the house, Sadie's father takes advantage of her presence to relieve the nurse who takes care of her mother. "Can you stay for an hour or so? I'm going to go pick up a few things." He says this so naturally, as if it were their usual arrangement, as if she were there every week, at the usual time, to look after her mother who no longer knows how to look after herself. She stays, she upholds the arrangement.

Her father leaves and she makes herself a cup of tea in the kitchen. It's clearly her father who does the cooking. The pantry is well stocked. He has taken over. Physical health is a concern he does not neglect.

A voice breaks through the quiet of the house and makes Sadie jump: "Oh, I'm sorry, dear. I didn't mean to startle you...Have you seen the young man, dear?" "You mean, Dad? Your husband? The one who lives here?" "No, no! Not the older gentleman who lives here. No, the young man, who comes to see me. He's very nice, you know. We take walks together. He takes me out to dinner sometimes. Very handsome." "Ah...I think he went out..." "Oh, good. Well, when he comes back, tell him I'm ready to go out. He's very nice, very kind. He's a med student, he's going to be a surgeon, I met him at the university. He's very serious, but he's very passionate." "Okay, I'll tell him when I see him…" "Thank you, dear."

Her mother is still standing in the middle of the kitchen, smiling politely, with a naïveté that doesn't quite fit with the composure she has maintained despite everything. She can't situate herself in relation to this kind visitor, achieve the appropriate level of familiarity. Sadie can't help but notice the excitement on her mother's face, which she thinks she's hiding as she leaves the room again. Her mother has come home in another timeline. She has met the young Dr. X again. They have no kids, they have time to rewrite history. In the new youth of senility, Sadie has been cancelled, she too is liberated a little from her ancestry. Her mother has gone soft in the head, but the new delirium is almost interesting to Sadie. She almost wants to follow her mother, to go upstairs to the bedrooms, to find the thread that was always missing in her story. She glimpsed, in her mother's expression, something of what she once saw in her.

While the tea leaves steep in the cup of boiling water, Sadie thinks back to a conversation she'd had a few years earlier at a virology conference in Austin with American researchers who were working on the measles virus. They had just presented the results of a long study that had allowed them to demonstrate that the virus could erase the immunological memory of the organism it infected, an amnesia that stripped the body of knowledge of previous viral interactions. Something electric had happened in that auditorium at the University of Texas, from which the researchers, despite their academic equanimity, could not completely protect themselves. Sadie too let herself get swept up in that terrible excitement, because yes, it was terrible, the power of the virus, but the regulatory intelligence was also just so impressive. It went further than simple parasitic opportunism. It was partly evolutionary chance, of course. Sadie knew how to temper her own enthusiasm. The intelligence that presented itself to her was not a plan, but something even better, an ability to adapt to the new, to the unreasonable diversity of the world. Still, it was undeniable; knowing how to rewrite the body's past was a rather powerful thing.

The telephone rings, startling her again. "Sadie? It's Claire Jean-Baptiste, from the lab at the Hôtel-Dieu. Listen, maybe I should mind my own business, but I wanted to tell you... We have the equipment here, for the genome sequencing. You could do it here." Sadie is thrown off by her directness, she stammers a little before getting a hold of herself. "Well, like I said, the plan is for me to go back to Marseille for the sequencing."

"Yes, that's what you said. I'm really sorry... But allow me to insist. I know you planned to leave again. But I just want to say, I really think you should do it here. And I would like to do it with you."

Sadie hangs up after stuttering something further, she'll think about it, she said, to buy time. She remains surprised by the woman's aplomb. She doesn't really know why she didn't just politely refuse. She pours the tea, the infuser forgotten in the pot, and takes a bitter sip.

X X

A virus does not divide like a cell, from one mother cell to two daughter cells. The virus does not have that loyalty to cellular reproduction. Its reproduction, its presence everywhere in the world, is therefore necessarily due to a stupid, repetitive, pre-sexual proliferation. Like the living dead, it can explode anytime, anywhere.

This is what a renowned Marxist philosopher explained to Sadie about two years ago when she met him at an official ceremony where Régnier was being honoured. She had read his books, she admired his thinking. It was so unpleasant, she'd thought, when someone whose intelligence you appreciate steps outside of their field of expertise and suddenly becomes a mediocre blowhard.

"Listen, human life is of an extreme insignificance, it is utterly contingent. It can be wiped out by a chance happening as silly as a virus. Or an asteroid."

At her age, Sadie is hardened to mediocre blowhards. The ones who talk over her in oily voices, when they don't just outright ignore her and talk among themselves, just slightly over her head. When she first arrived in France, at the beginning of her research career, she would still make an effort. She thought it was a question of knowledge, accreditation, she thought that if they didn't recognize genius, they would surely recognize the language of objective data. After a few years, she came to understand this had nothing to do with it. If she managed to get their attention for a moment, it was because they were taking a break from their masculine battles, thinking, oh look, how cute, and she's trying to think too!

She can't pinpoint exactly when her status went from sweetheart to spinster. It's been a long time since she tried to make herself heard, since she stopped fighting for a spot in the ring, but she continued to listen to them, to stand there, bogged down in the grease of their unctuous voices. Before even the slightest sign of interest or curiosity can be expressed, they unleash the soliloquy that's been brewing between the impermeable walls of their aging male solitude. That is what makes them so impossible to escape in those eternal moments: in their odorous, distinguished eloquence lies all the pain they are unable to honour, the impoverished pain of being alone in the world that has remained frozen inside them, the silent witness continually ignored by the court of their critical discourse. She is enveloped by their pain in that moment, she is the only one to hear it and she cannot get away. When the moment passes, she tells herself that next time she will cut things short before any rapport is established, she replays the irritating episode and imagines, next time, communicating her refusal with a laconic gesture and marching off with no remorse to the other side of the room.

XX

Claire Jean-Baptiste and Sadie are sitting across from one another waiting for the computer to analyze the sample. The process involves a lot of waiting around as the machine recognizes what is unreadable to the human eye. Claire has a round face with round eyes that widen as she speaks. Her hair is in braids that reach her shoulders. She's playing Martha Wainwright in the lab, which surprises Sadie, who expected something more electronic given the young woman's style. Claire tells her that this was the first CD she bought when she arrived from Haiti in the early 2000s. She would walk around the city listening to it on repeat, as if it would help her learn to live here.

"Martha gave me a language to understand Montreal. There's a kind of strength in her sadness."

Claire had walked the interminable streets, but she didn't manage to feel like she was part of the city. They had told her that the transition from Port-au-Prince to Montreal would be easy because of the French. Everything was arranged so that she'd have a place to stay at first, with an aunt she didn't know. Her father made frequent trips to Quebec and had told her all about it. Claire had dreamed of a big North American city, but Montreal turned out to be disarmingly simple, she could walk the same street from north to south for hours without ever losing her way. And yet, she felt like this city, the one she couldn't break away from, was only an impermeable layer preventing her from accessing a more intimate experience of the place. The different neighbourhoods functioned like little villages, where people stayed close to home, never venturing too far except when necessary. Her aunt, for example, only left her neighbourhood in the north of the city to take the bus that dropped her at the door of the hospital where she worked as a nurse. Claire had imagined that by leaving her island, she would find a place where lives intermingled, bumping up against one another and reinventing themselves through that contact, she'd imagined that in the cold, anonymous chaos of the great northern cities, the sun would not weigh so heavily on each person's destiny. She found the cold, but also therein a surprising absence of the chaos and the unpredictable company of strangers she'd hoped for. For the first few years, she spent most of her time with people from Haiti, all of whom had a more or less immediate connection to her own culture, and she was unable to break through to anyone outside of the community that had taken her in. At university, she made a few polite acquaintances with other students, but it took her years to develop any deeper relationships. Years before anyone invited her home to dinner. She just glided along on an affected benevolence, she could see people observing themselves being friendly, she could see them calculating the amplitude of their smile, conjuring up an enthusiasm as they questioned her about her background. On the street, in the city's many cafés, and even at night in the bars, young Montrealers moved with the confidence of those who are not seeking to meet anyone new, those who have already found what they need in life. It was only while doing her PhD at McGill, only by crossing to the other side of the mountain and into the world of research, that Claire met other students who, like her, were looking for something else. "Anyway, if it weren't for Martha, I wouldn't have been able to stay here," Claire says, as Wainwright's fatigue washes over the room in waves.

"Martha belonged to this place, this city, but I felt a kind of suffering in her that I couldn't find anywhere else. She was nothing like me, and that's what I was looking for, something that was totally different but that would still speak to me a little. She let me believe in the possibility of finding the city somewhere. Otherwise, I would have just moved to Toronto or Vancouver."

Claire talks a lot. Sadie rests a little in the flood of her words, which is suspended for a moment as Claire rolls her chair toward one of the computers. There's something of Molly in her, the way she orchestrates the whole world for herself alone, but with a radical absence of the calculated way Molly presents herself to others. Sadie can feel the connection already forming between her nervous system and Claire's. She feels it when it happens, it's never a question of time, it's never gradual, the bond that grows out of that connection at the speed of sensitive nerve endings.

Claire's way of talking about Montreal touches Sadie, it appeals to her, the way Claire moves from one image to the next, the associations created so freely in her mind and then formulated with the same fervour. The air softens, an indifference gradually mutes Sadie's senses. Painkillers sent by the security system of her psyche. That's what happens when she gets too close. A detachment beyond her control. She listens to Claire speak, she tries to connect with the meaning of her words. Claire looks Sadie right in the eye and punctuates her statements with her name, as if to remind her that she is right there, in front of her. She calls out to Sadie, and Sadie stays and keeps staying. At first, the intensity of her words makes Sadie doubt that she is indeed their intended recipient, there must have been a mistake. But each time she says Sadie, looking directly in her eyes. Each time, she brings her a little further out of her torpor, her name, Sadie, spoken by Claire, with her accent, surprises Sadie, sends a little shock to her nervous system, and she strings the moment back onto the chain. Word by word, through the revelation of Claire's voice, Sadie holds on. In the profusion of her own name, the inexplicable, unreasonable generosity with which Claire addresses her and tells Sadie her story, a space opens up.

Sadie listens, and an energy begins to flow through her. Then Claire falls silent. The troop of machines have reached the end of the sequence.

X X

Working with giant viruses has forced Sadie to become accustomed to not knowing what she's looking at. There's no doubt that this is a Pandoravirus, but there are an impressive number of genes in the sequence of capital letters strung together to identify the virus in our language that are unlike anything we know in the living world.

It no longer shocks her as much as it once did. But when they compare their analyses with the results of other members of *Pandoraviridae,* what's surprising is the number of genes in this new virus that don't come from the same family. Because there is a family, a Pandora family, and this virus belongs to it, that much is undeniable. These genes whose lineage cannot be traced are called orphans. This leads to one of the thorniest questions posed by the Pandoras, which, from an evolutionary point of view, have in common a staggering number of genes for which there is no known counterpart in nature: where do all these orphans come from?

When Régnier and Sadie discovered the first specimens, they presumed, as common sense would dictate, that they were the offspring of a common ancestor that hadn't survived, a truly gigantic progenitor that could have contained all of these genes before breaking down and losing its form. Evolution is not sentimental; it pays little attention to the individual envelope. What matters is genetic survival. There is a still widespread idea that viruses originate in the cell, that they are its degenerated descendants. A degraded morsel of life that would hang onto the memory of its original cellular form. It would explain why they carry the code of the living. Those fallen descendants would have become parasites of life out of nostalgia for the abundance their ancestors had known, seeking reunion with life by infecting it. But, for Sadie, this crypto-Platonism ignores the real-life evidence unearthed over the last few years, that is, the considerable size of giant viruses. The theory presupposes the presence of ancestors with a genetic baggage large enough to contain the growing number of unknown genes found in current specimens.

The more Régnier and Sadie expanded the nomenclature of the *Pandoraviridae,* discovering increasingly enormous members, the more difficult it became to work solely on the assumption of a particularly venerable extinct ancestor. It's not easy for humans to accept the idea that genes can be transmitted in any way other than vertically, from the past to the future, via an ancestor. The idea of genetic material not being passed down by descendants seems unnatural, it throws off the archetypal image of the tree of life. Humans don't take kindly to interference with cherished images, Sadie knows that all too well. If we take away the idea of the family tree, how will they talk about their origins?

How will they conceive of their own past if they can no longer imagine themselves at the bottom of a vertical structure, where each present derives from an anteriority that explains its existence?

The genomic identification leaves no room for doubt, this is definitely another member of the Pandoravirus family, but its genes don't correspond to anything else known. In the same family, the code took completely new paths. Inside the virus, substances are transforming in an unprecedented way. There must be an error somewhere. Sadie and Claire agree, they go over the results again, they align the databases. Sadie can see that Claire, bustling from one machine to another, takes it seriously. She's invested. As they go back over everything, as they try to locate the error, a feverish anxiety grows, an energy that runs counter to the correction process. They don't need to look at each other to feel it. They check everything, the results, the analyses, the data from the machines, but they know what they saw. Completely new genes.

The room is almost trembling with energy that wants to coagulate toward the obvious. Sadie tries to stabilize the situation, mostly to avoid jumping to hasty conclusions, to control the churning, the small spasms of her digestive system. The facts want to assemble into a hypothesis. With each new member of the family, new genes. She can feel Claire getting carried away next to her, she can already hear that she is about to say her name, break the loaded silence, she can already feel Claire's voice touching her, as her words come together, as her thoughts associate, clashing in an effort to unite, before Sadie can prevent the contact. The idea has already found a way.

It's as if the virus were inventing its own code, its own language.

XX

When Sadie gets back to the hotel, she goes straight to the enormous black-tiled shower. The hot water scorches her skin. She lets it run for a long time, without interruption. In a small brown plastic bottle, she finds a liquid with a surprising scent, a woodsy dominant note, a strong musk colliding with a smoky base note of dried flowers. A compound concocted in a lab to allow the men passing through these rooms to access the essence of a virility they wouldn't achieve on their own.

When she travels with Régnier, they never stay in luxurious places. Their style is more minimalist camping, grim hotels with rough plaster walls. Sadie hadn't put too much thought into booking a hotel this time, her plans were made quickly, she looked for something downtown, she wanted something big to act as a buffer between her and the city. When she made the reservation, she hadn't imagined herself in such a trendy place. Yet she knew this hotel once. She gets out of the shower and pulls on the hotel bathrobe, lets the thick fabric gently dry her skin. She folds down the bedspread on the king-size bed and slips under the silky sheets stretched over the mattress by an experienced hand. She smooths the dense, almost liquid percale with her fingertips, with the soles of her feet.

They gave her a room with a very nice view, carefully calculated to enhance the uplifting and reassuring effect of Montreal's geometric layout. A few metres below, McGill College Avenue stretches out in a straight line to the base of Mount Royal, the campus of the prestigious university unfurling between these two points, the promenade with the majestic Arts Building, and behind it, English-style facades covered with vines that climb the mountainside, with the Faculty of Medicine at the summit. A steady rise toward excellence.

The chateau-like style of the university mirrors Sadie's hotel, named for the Queen—the last of the grand railway hotels built since the nineteenth century by Canadian rail companies to dot the crossing, from east to west, of the New World. The Canadians could only attempt to reinvent America by taking as a model a kind of European grandeur that was already doomed to decay, a fading dream of opulence. Where the American Old West was colonized by barbaric cowboys, Canada sent in the calvary to ensure the law of the Ancien Régime would reign over this immense unknown land. While King Ludwig II of Bavaria was going for broke building Neuschwanstein Castle, his very own Versailles on the impassible heights of sacred mountains, already dreaming of hosting Wagner and breathing the same air as the gods, Canada was busy recreating its own neo-versions of European chateaux from one end of the country to the other. In the middle of a vast wilderness and in the centre of cities yet to be built, travellers from the Canadian elite would discover new versions of what they had left behind, reproducing the only ideas of wealth and prestige they were able to imagine. As her gaze lingers on the cruciform skyscraper at Place Ville Marie, Sadie suddenly remembers that her hotel is not actually one of these Canadian chateaux, as she had been imagining in the last few minutes, but instead a work of rigorously modern architecture, standing in contrast to the other beads in the rosary, rejecting all ornamentation and all romanticism. She finds it very strange to have made this mistake, to catch herself believing she's standing in the last offshoot, the final stop on this return to the past, when she knows very well that the Queen's Hotel, like its neighbours, was born of an ambition to present Montreal as a city of the future, an ambition embodied in what they called the international style, an odd name now that she thinks about it, which had attempted to imagine progress by borrowing from interwar Europe, its dream of crude, objective, functional durability.

How could she have imagined herself in such mannered, kitschy romanticism, when she was actually standing behind a facade she knew so well, one built in a unified, highly rational block? She'd been thinking she was in Quebec City, maybe, a few hours up the river, at the Château Frontenac, where her father had taken her when she was ten years old on a trip to meet with the upper echelons of the Nationalist Party. He'd booked a suite in the Riverview Wing, where she slept on the pullout. As her mother's stand-in, Sadie accompanied her father to gatherings in the ballroom and to breakfast in front of the big, cinematic windows. The rest of the time, she was on her own, wandering the corridors, strolling the long path overlooking the cape. Quebec City felt like a movie set to her. On the last day, after his meetings, Sadie's father, electrified by the rousing speeches, marched her down to the old town to show her what an authentic French-Canadian city looked like. He didn't mention that most of the former French colony had undergone a twenty-year reconstruction, and that the final touches had just been put on an erasure of the previous two centuries, and, more importantly, the eradication of any trace of English style left on the cradle of French America. She only learned that decades later, when she had a brief fling with an American lighting designer who had worked on the set of a blockbuster film shot in the old city. It was a convenient location for period films, cheaper than France and in pristine condition.

The Queen's Hotel has recently been fully renovated, renewing its aspirations to modernity. The old ballrooms, where the actual Queen had danced, have given way to coworking labs, multipurpose spaces bearing names that evoke Silicon Valley instead of Versailles or Balmoral. Walking around the deserted floor home to the "CoLab," where she sees only hotel staff, in the perfect crystallization of an already obsolete present, Sadie almost misses the imitation of the past. In any case, she tells herself, she's horrified by all of it, the decadent way these people live. She's there as a renegade, she hates this, she tells herself over and over in the elevator, as if to keep that world at a distance.

At the hotel restaurant, the server is scrupulously polite, she only clocks his hostility when she follows him with her eyes as he leaves the table and sees him suddenly drop his pleasant expression. She is grateful to him for the affected care that protects her from the familiarity of the city, out there, just beyond the hotel walls. The restaurant has also been given a facelift, with shiny new surfaces everywhere that reflect the light that glides and shimmers, except the soft velvet of the chairs, which generously absorbs all matter—flesh, scents, sounds—entering its purple proximity. The architect was clearly given a mission to eliminate any hint of the old space. Not a trace remains of the restaurant that hosted the Royal Sunday Brunch, the kitschy antique decor that was, at the time, the definition of chic. For someone who hated the Queen of England and everything associated with her, and who had still not recovered from the failure of the petition to name the hotel Château Maisonneuve upon its inauguration in 1958, in honour of the city's French heritage, Sadie's father had loved to take his family to the royal brunch, with no ulterior motive. The Queen's Hotel became a favourite destination for her father's rare gastronomic overindulgences. The man who proudly Gallicized everything, who wouldn't even say "7 Up," insisting on ordering a "Sept haut," was remarkably cheerful, almost floating, in the midst of the abundance of English sauce, smoked salmon and trout, braised ham, meat pies, oeufs mayonnaise. That man, who normally kept a strict diet, which was by extension imposed on all members of the family, seemed to rediscover beef Wellington each time they went. The Royal Sunday Brunch at the Queen's Hotel was a day of celebration. For a few hours at least. Back at home, his enthusiasm quickly waned, his digestion would catch up with his zeal, and Sadie's father would spend the rest of the afternoon soaking in a hot bath to help "unclog the pipes." He would rage against the trifle, the Stilton, the beef cheek that was much fattier than usual. When he came out, mollified by an hour and a half in the tub, he would go straight to bed without a word to anyone.

Today, not a trace of that restaurant remains. Sadie can't even figure out its original location, the hotel layout no longer aligns with her memories. She suddenly wonders if she could manage to not leave the hotel again, to reserve a return flight immediately and live in this recycled air until her departure was imminent, if she could manage to not take another breath of the outside, saturated with memories, with far too much of the known, and taking her system by storm.

She needs to get out of here as fast as possible, yes, and take her virus back to the old world. She can feel the urgency pressing down on her body. Régnier will not hold her silence against her, he'll understand that things got a little out of hand. Go home, this time to the only home that counts, the one she chose, and forget these last few days.

But as she looks down at her fillet of snapper, Claire's voice comes back to her, the little electric shock that summons Sadie. The voice returns and sows mild panic in the hollow of her entrails, just a little light intestinal activity, she thinks, it will pass. Sadie, the voice says, projecting itself toward her, a light but deliberate gesture. Sadie, punctuating its sentences sharply. It makes no sense, she tries again to ignore this feeling, but it persists. She concentrates on the plate in front of her, tries to regain the calm of rigidity, she focuses on the image of the dainty white fish, its simplicity helps her straighten her spine, tense the muscles of her belly, her back, compress herself around the main axis of her body. She pulls her fork through the white flesh, which flakes apart easily, it disintegrates in her mouth, nothing like her father's royal feasts, meats oozing fat, the cheeses veined with blue mould, *Penicillium*, she wonders if he has been back since the reopening, no, for her just white fish, some leeks with vinaigrette. No sauce, she was careful to specify, Sadie never overdoes it.

She was a little chubby as a child, roundish, her mother would say, it was her personal resistance against the militant diet imposed by her father. He was compact and sinewy, and her mother svelte and lithe. Among the children, it was easy to separate those who adhered, body and soul, to the parental regime—the thin ones— from those who had found somewhere inside themselves the strength to resist through fat. Sadie's father and her oldest brother, François, skinny and mean, called her Fatso. When she got home from school, Sadie would sneak into the kitchen, where she would crack an egg into a bowl and add a spoonful of butter and a little sugar. She would gulp down this mucus, her insides torn between the fear of her mother's sudden appearance and the insubordination of a rebellious appetite. She didn't even have to chew, the slimy mixture slid straight down her throat into her stomach. Her mother must have suspected something, Sadie must have left traces, because she sometimes included in her sermons, when lecturing on the theme of a healthy mind in a healthy body, a note about the dangers of eating in secret. The only thing worse than stuffing your face was hiding away to do it. Sadie is careful not to imagine too vividly the horror her mother must have felt seeing her daughter shovelling down that foul magma of sugar and fat, a paralyzing horror that prevented her from even interrupting the abject scene.

Sadie's mother had no personal experience of the feeling of flabby skin, the dampness of chafing thighs, the inescapability of a protruding belly. Her own mother had put her in boarding school at the age of five, at the convent across the street, so she had no time to take it easy in childhood, she was whipped into shape early. The official reason for sending the child away was that her mother, who assisted her doctor husband on his many visits, was too busy to take care of her own offspring. Discipline had shaped her mother's small body. People who have always been thin can't help it, they're revolted by fat. It becomes a moral issue. Sadie's mother, who was raised Protestant, had absorbed the idea of predestination. Being thin was her way of convincing herself that she had been chosen to lead a life of impeccable righteousness. Anyone who deviated from corporal discipline was necessarily suspect.

Neither mother nor father could digest anything, they lived in such a state of continual tension that it tied their intestines in knots. The household menu consisted of a few variations on a limited number of dishes that wouldn't inflame the digestive tract. They did not stoop to junk, greasy fare that betrayed an inferior nature. The only exception was the royal brunch and, under normal circumstances, it went unmentioned. As soon as Sadie crossed the threshold of that house for the last time, she started to lose weight. She arrived in France in December and was sick with anxiety all winter, exhausted from having so easily violated the ban on leaving. Alone in her tiny studio in Marseille, where the walls were beading with damp, where the wind rushed in and couldn't blow back out so that it was often colder inside than out in the fresh air, she imagined her parents dying from her blasphemous act, she saw them writhing, bruised by an unexpectedly brutal pain. She hadn't been able to proclaim her rejection, announce her defection, she had never, in her whole life with this family, been able to repel their madness. Withdrawing was available to her, so she withdrew. They continued to lead the same life they had led until then, in the same amount of pain. Nobody dwelled on the significance of her departure, they simply shifted the ban on leaving to a ban on any mention of the pariah's name.

When, six months later, she emerged from her state of shock, she discovered a strange new body, and all the sensations that came with it. Her affliction had stripped her of her curves, and her pain had melted away with the fat. She had not noticed herself losing weight, she had spent months scrambling around, charging through the city like a madwoman. One day she woke up and was astonished to touch her thighs, her belly, her waist, and find a new density, as if her body, which she had always known to be stooped and hunched, had focused on itself by straightening up. There had been a shift in its defensive posture, Sadie was armoured now, she was on the offensive.

Her cravings, too, had changed. It was strange to look at the cakes, pastries, and charcuterie that had been forbidden in her parents' house and feel unmoved. Once she would have indulged at any opportunity, but now she felt void of any longing for these aggregates of sugar and fat. Her organism had found another morphology and reprogrammed itself, activating some thinness gene that had lain dormant up till then. When she passed by the butcher shop, or when someone offered her a profiterole, she noticed the complete absence of attraction, a total silencing of desire. She felt like she had been reformatted to live the life of great slenderness that had always seemed inaccessible.

She took a previously unknown pleasure in witnessing this winnowing away of her mass, she delighted in occupying space as she had never done before. She experimented with new postures that had been too ridiculous to even try out in her former body. Since childhood, she had preserved in memory a composite gestural language, carefully noted the positions she admired in the graceful silhouettes that seemed to belong to another kingdom of the living. She contorted herself in the mirror, trying out every angle, just for the pleasure of knocking herself off-kilter, making the rows of ribs appear underneath her skin, she liked to see her skeleton. With the appearance of her bones and the contours of a new musculature, the traits of a certain type of femininity were erased, features she had worn without ever fully possessing them. As her fat melted away, it redrew the curve of her hips, her ass, recast the line of her breasts. The new experience of her torso did not displease her. As with everything else, she got used to it. Her acquired thinness stopped seeming like a miracle, grew muffled by familiarity, and Sadie stopped projecting herself into space.

X

It should have all been very simple. Round trip. Arrive, stay long enough to grab the virus, and set sail again. Burst back in, but just barely, really more like a bounce, a streak, a flash of lightning instantly vanishing. Besides, she has responsibilities, she can't just do whatever she wants, she has ties, which she has chosen very carefully, by the way, according to her very limited capacity for settling down. Everywhere she goes, she unfailingly locates the exit. Never again will she find herself stuck. Right now, she's really not enjoying this illegible, incoherent feeling of a certain activity, the first fizz of an effervescence, maybe, that threatens to keep her in place. The unstable movement of a heavy weight. In her mind, Claire's voice mingles with the lines of capital letters that make up the code of the virus. An urgent need to defecate, unrelated to her digestion, which is regular and dependable. How is it possible that one member of a family has so little in common with the rest? Where did all these genes come from? What is this thing that seems to have appeared out of nothing? Sadie has a feeling that the more she learns about the virus, the more it tells her about itself, the less sense it will make.

Sadie, says Claire, again and again, and her voice is agitating in every direction.

XX

Sadie leaves the Queen's Hotel early in the morning to head to the lab at the Hôtel-Dieu. It's not very far so she decides to walk, and the feeling of descending deeper and deeper into the entrails of the city makes her queasy. The hospital is on Saint-Paul, in the heart of Old Montreal, the site of its founding in 1645 by Jeanne Mance, who would run the place for thirty years. Sadie is amazed at how much of the city's geography has stayed with her all these years. Montreal has certainly evolved, but the bones of it have remained the same.

Claire sent her a text, she's waiting in the lab. She seemed keyed up. Sadie can sense that she's coming up on something big, she always knows when she's getting close to an important discovery, when something is about to be unlocked, she can feel it coming. It's the resistance she encounters. There is a stiffness in the feeling of imminence—when the stability of her world is about to be shaken up, a stiffness sets in, a last bulwark against upheaval, which is expressed with the words: "Is she going to make it?" She already knows, she saw it in the first analyses, something is off, there's something there that doesn't fit with her understanding of the situation, something that eludes her as she gets closer, she can see it but doesn't yet know what it is she's seeing. Somewhere inside her, an impending change has already been reported, the news is circulating in the system. A whole bunch of mechanisms have been set in motion, every time it's the same thing, and it's the clear reaction of these inner alarm systems that warns her. Incidentally, this is also the way a virus that has penetrated and infected a human organism makes itself known. The virus has already made its way into the cells and is sometimes quite far along in its reproduction process before its presence is detected by the brain. The immune system gets upset and expresses the infection. In the same way, it's when Sadie starts to feel her psychic defence system freaking out, gets the sense that forces are working a little too hard to restore homeostasis, that she suspects that the virus is about to teach her something she's absolutely not prepared to learn. Will she rise to the occasion? Is she going to make it? She walks down the wide boulevard alongside her hotel. It's quite early, Saturday morning, not a soul in the street. There's nothing to block the wind between the rows of skyscrapers and it bounces back off the walls. Sadie hunches her shoulders up around her ears, tries as best she can to shield herself from the blasts of frigid air.

She escapes the wind tunnel by turning right onto the big hill that leads to the southern part of the island. Montreal is steep; she'd forgotten. Her feet are propelled forward, she has to lean back, maintain her centre of gravity to stay upright. The ground is covered with tiny pebbles that are meant to provide a grip on the sidewalk, but she never knows when she'll hit a patch of ice. Since her arrival, she's had to be prepared for anything. The incline does force her to straighten out her spine. As she's pulled down the slippery hill, she resists, stiffens, and then, to avoid collapsing, lets herself be carried down the slope. Each time her foot hits the ground, it jolts her whole body, she can feel it in her joints, even her sight lurches. She'll soon be at the river, not that she can see it from here. It's easy to forget that Montreal is an island when you're there, all the years she was away she imagined the city like a distant island, enclosed in the parentheses of an unpleasant memory, she chose to live in a city where the sea is always right there, reminding her that she can get away anytime she wants to, whispering to her that elsewhere is close by. Marseille is a steep city too, she is always either making the controlled effort to climb or hurtling toward an ocean that could swallow her up and sweep her far away, the divisions between city and sea are lost, in this descent where each step shakes her whole body, she's already kind of there, on her way toward the open sea, she tries to slow down but she can't anymore, she's afraid of falling forward, being dragged down and tumbling headlong, unstoppable, she's walking down the hill but she can't see the water, Montreal cannot quite believe that it's an island, will the city ever manage to open up, all the pieces collide in a jerky, broken rhythm, the ground slides beneath her, the little pebbles roll under her boots, Montreal is unravelling beneath her feet, but like the turn of a kaleidoscope, each jolt dismantles and then reassembles the city in a single twist, with the same material. Montreal is always remaking itself from the same debris.

When she finally reaches the bottom of the hill, she stops for a moment. Her eyes are wet with tears, they spill down her cheeks, she feels a deep fatigue moving through her. She's exhausted, from what has happened or what is to come, she's not sure, she needs a moment to gather herself, but Claire is waiting, the lab is ready. She starts walking again, sends some energy back to her legs, her chest, she propels herself forward so as not to collapse.

X

When Sadie arrives at the lab, Claire greets her with uncontained excitement. The last readings of the genome have been translated into amino acid sequences. They're about to find out what it's made of, which proteins are involved. Claire doesn't hide her pride, because even for Sadie, who works in a lab designed for these kinds of operations, which are far from a priority in a hospital, this is an impressive turnaround. This tells Sadie that Claire's power of influence doesn't work only on her. As Sadie quickly glances over the results, she realizes there's something more behind Claire's triumphant look.

For most people, protein is little more than a number on a yogurt tub. But in Sadie's world, each protein is a universe. Proteins play a specific role and tell her, for example, whether the virus she's looking at can leap onto her and find a home base in her system. Those microscopic arrangements allow us to begin to understand the infection strategy a virus has developed, and it's by speaking protein that the virus enters our world. And, it must be said, the virus speaks this protein language quite elegantly. When presented with an unknown host, the virus can develop a protein that responds precisely to the entry code of one of the cells of that particular host. The virus evolves its own form along the way. Faced with a closed door, it learns to speak the language of the guard. Some might call this opportunism, but Sadie sees it as a magnificent capacity for innovation and adaptation. Because the virus doesn't just change sides based on affinity. It puts effort and work into crossing the intermediary space that separates it from the right key, by trial and error. It is fundamentally transformed by its encounters. It would be easy to think that the propensity for change is just what a parasite does—it makes sense to adapt to others when you're living at their expense. But to immediately reduce the virus to the status of parasite overlooks something important: what it is to inhabit the world by association, to evolve on the planet by taking the time to understand—from the inside—those we meet along the way.

X

Sadie's eyes fly over the screen, taking in the clusters of capital letters produced by the translation. Each sequence identifies the structure of a protein from the genome. She moves from one group to the next, looking for a familiar sequence. With the programs she has in Marseille, she'll be able to make more refined models, recreate the structure of the protein in space. But she doesn't even need to bother with that level of sophistication, she already knows that the sequences appearing on the digital read-out are unlike anything else. The first obvious fact is that the family now has a new member.

To translate the DNA of the virus into protein, you need to give it time to reproduce. The virus can't tell us about its function in a language we understand. Only once it has completed at least one cycle of infection can we collect the material needed to make sense of it. It is precisely in that space of a few hours, a complete cycle, a small revolution, that Sadie stops agreeing with her fellow scientists. For most of them, the infection time is precisely what allows the virus to penetrate the living being, to invade it, colonize it. It's once the virus hijacks a living cell that we can reckon with it and agree to negotiate. And technically, it's the infected cell we confer with. We're only really interested in it once it knows how to talk proteins and performance, once it reveals its mode of operation so we can get rid of it, that's generally its only utility. Without that process, the virus is just a dirty parasite, a terrorist. And we all know by now that you don't negotiate with terrorists.

During the infection cycle, the virus learns to speak our language. Once inside, it uses our code to make its signs speak. It does have signs, genes, it's made up of them too. But its signature only becomes legible once it has access to the tools for decoding it. At that point, in our eyes at least, it starts doing something. Before then, it's not even a terrorist, just a bomb waiting to go off to break through the walls of the living. Without the breach into our world, there's little chance the virus will be acknowledged, that it will tell us anything, that we will reckon with it anymore than we would a rock. And it's here that Sadie diverges from her colleagues' opinions, breaks with the human camp.

Seeing this stage of infection means witnessing a metamorphosis that never fails to move her. Witnessing this—that is, moving beyond the idea of successive steps like inert photographs of an unsurprising progression, and instead following what's actually happening—is to see the very notion of boundaries, and of passage through them, become incoherent. There's no going back; what was once placed in the small column of the category "virus" has escaped it, its reality will now never stop spilling over the squared-off box of the concept, and the very outline of its name starts to blur.

To monitor an infecting virus is to watch a creature master a new language in just a few hours. And now, in this Montreal lab, this one is ready to speak Sadie's language. Except something strange has happened in the translation process. The bioinformatics program, which acts as an interpreter between the viral world and our own, has produced an analysis in which most of the genes are translated into proteins that have no known function. Claire has checked everything, it's not a translation problem, the solution wasn't lost along the way. The genes have been properly translated into proteins, but the proteins have no recognizable signature, nothing that can be associated with a precise function in our world. They're what are called orphan proteins. Sadie had been prepared for this possibility, as with the other Pandora viruses. It's the shared trait of this large and atypical family of giant viruses— the proteins travel in the virus's genetic baggage and we have no idea what they're doing there, we're unable to ascribe any usefulness to the particles whose usefulness is their very reason for being.

But what's bothering Sadie is that, this time, these free riders apparently make up the bulk of the virus. If she considers the genes that belong to this individual alone, leaving out what it has in common with the other members of its family, she's looking at almost ninety-five percent. This is unheard of. The proportion of this virus's proteins that could tell us anything about its function in the world is incredibly small. Each virus teaches Sadie how to study it. She's used to being flexible, adapting to their singular style. But this time, the shared vocabulary she could use to learn to speak its language is limited.

The Pandora viruses, as a community, are distinguished by the fact that they ultimately have very little in common with each other. Their affiliation lies in their ability to set themselves apart from their family of origin. And that's what Sadie is having a hard time grasping: their mode of replication that has nothing to do with loyalty to the genes that made us. Because that is what links us, biologically, to our family as humans, animals, plants, bacteria—loyalty to the gene. It's a flattering way of looking at things, from the point of view of a given organism. In truth, each of us is first and foremost a transitory vehicle for information passed from generation to generation, from copy to copy. We living beings are nothing more than temporary machines ensuring the survival of a code. If we look at it this way, our own characters, which we consider so essential, so significant, are simply the ephemeral, finite expression of information transmitted through time—with a few errors and mutations along the way—with a fairly impressive rate of fidelity.

X

It happens every time, Sadie gives herself a horrible backache after hunching over for hours to watch the spectacle of metamorphosis, every part of her body tensed and stretched toward the unexpected. She could easily spare her vertebrae, watch the process on the computer screen that faithfully relays the image, but she can't help herself, it's part of her ritual. Taking part in the infection cycle of a new virus is like witnessing the birth of a child, without the anxiety of knowing that another human being has been brought into the world.

Every time, she emerges from this process miserable, unable to straighten up, bent over like an old lady with a twisted spine, sometimes she actually has to use a cane to walk for days afterward, it's as if she's been there for years, contorting her spine, as if the tension of her excitement had cost her decades of good health. And maybe that's what really happens, she lives at the accelerated rhythm of the virus, which completes a life cycle every twelve hours on average, because it is a whole life cycle that unfolds before her very eyes. She takes part in the life of the virus as an amazed observer. And this life cannot be reduced to the visible box of the virus. The virus is the collection of phenomena that are produced in the infection. The virus is not the bomb, it is the explosion of life that shatters the limits of the individual. In that transformation, the infectious life alters the concepts Sadie has inherited to define the phenomenon of the living.

The virus is not the box.

Perhaps this is what has always felt wrong to her about Régnier naming it Pandora, as if it were only a matter of opening a box, as if life could be explained in terms of containers. Yet it was Régnier, when she met him, who showed her how the world of viruses would dismantle everything, right down to the containers. With the discovery of the *Pandoraviridae*, he opened the box of what had been understood until then as truth, and transferred the new reality to a new box, with a new name. He was the one who had cautioned her from the beginning against those for whom the power of science could be summed up like that, the power of opening a box only to place its contents into a new box, and especially the prerogative of sticking a name on it. Knowing how to handle the hazardous potential, moving it from one container to another, taking care to wash your hands when leaving the lab, disposing of protective equipment in designated bins.

It's not the first time that Sadie has discovered a new member without him. But she's far away. She still hasn't contacted him in the three days she's been here. Claire has followed the process, she notices Sadie's distress. "So," she asks, "what do we do with this now?"

Sadie leaves Claire's question hovering in the air. She straightens up as best she can on her chair. Now, I take this back to Marseille. That's what she should say, but she can't get the words out. She's in bad shape, she makes a first attempt to get up, but the pain stops her short. It radiates down her legs and up to her neck, as she feels her muscles knot up in a chain reaction. It's more than a bad back this time, it's not just the tension in her spine that admonishes her, punishing her for having stayed so close to the miracle of transformations for so long, for having lived in the time of infection. Claire watches her calmly, saying nothing.

Sadie knows how to deal with back pain, the punishment suits her character, over time her entire physiognomy has been built around it. Each section knows its job, everything tightens at her shoulders and neck, tension accumulates where her strength resides and then gives way lower down. Many times Sadie saw her father paralyzed after very long operations, his lumbar curve deformed by hours spent bent over craniums with his hands in the convolutions of cervical flesh, his scalpel reading and rewriting cognitive matter. She's seen it: now he has a hard time straightening fully, he is growing less flexible with age, becoming stuck in that posture. Does Claire recognize the paternal defect in Sadie? Yes, Sadie has had role models. This was passed down to her, a certain way of breaking herself open, she was taught how to make herself the conduit of knowledge. What is undone in her will be reconstructed in nomenclatures, produce new forms that will give wonder to others. Claire is waiting, she's asking about the next step, but how can Sadie give her something she doesn't have? The protocol, the method, the computer sequencing, Claire knows all that, she doesn't need Sadie to show her what to do. She's learned well. What could Sadie have to offer?

What she needs her for is something of a different nature.

Okay, time to snap out of it, here's what she's going to do. She's going to get up and she's going to get out of here. It's time to end this little Montreal adventure, she should have left already. She tries to breathe deeply, lubricate her joints, but this time she feels the inflammation overtake her ability to adapt, shut down the possibility of movement.

She's taking so long to announce her departure that it's getting awkward, but when she finally turns to Claire to try to read her expression, she finds her surprisingly composed, waiting for Sadie without rushing her. There is an assurance in her patience, a discreet, knowing smile. In the space of the ever-expanding present, Claire makes a reversal seem possible. A series of reactions are triggered, spreading pain through her body. Claire still says nothing, nobody moves, but the apparent stillness is suffused with an ominous heat. Sadie can feel her nerves sizzling, and it seems to her, though she must be confused, that her inner turmoil is attuned to something coming from Claire. Fear usually plunges her into a defensive torpor that is suddenly slow to materialize. In its place, the pressure of a new demand, which Sadie is not sure she can meet, weighs heavily in her pelvis. But when she tries to relax, her lumbar vertebrae send out shockwaves of pain. Normally she'd do everything she could to contain and isolate the pain. But what she sees in Claire's face, tense with anticipation of what is about to happen, exerts a pull. Her symptoms are jostling her, telling her to turn back. She feels the imminence of an imbalance. But she also wants to see.

XX

The virus doesn't know how to translate. It has no ribosomes, those tiny reading machines present in every living being right down to the simplest bacteria. It's the ribosomes that decode the genes, more precisely the RNA, which is the messenger of DNA. Ribosomes read the code carried by the messenger and synthesize it in order to assemble the proteins that will allow the genetic code to come to life. Without those little decoders, the code would just sit there, illegible and useless. They're the ones who make something of it, who put it to work. Making genetic code into something functional is the skill shared by all recognized life forms on Earth.

Once upon a time, life flourished on the planet. Between six and five hundred million years ago, there was a prelude during which life emerged from independent systems, and then a great explosion—what we call the Cambrian explosion—a huge party where the life forms that had been coexisting in relative indifference until then broke apart for the first time and shattered the peace that had been reigning on Earth. Until then, everyone was just going about their business. Nobody cared much what the neighbours were doing; to each their own. There was no conflict, though not much harmony either. It was everyone for themselves. A quiet cacophony of solitary endeavours. And then, in this peaceful hubbub, there were a few encounters, communication was established thanks to a few accidents. Through their interactions, the solo artists of survival began to evolve. A great acceleration followed, and soon a big banquet, an intense festival from which arose a wealth of strategies for experimenting with life. These once solitary forms started associating, comparing strategies, and the collaboration paid off, a real boom in evolution. From the new aggregation a more and more competent generation emerged: multicellular life.

We living beings are all descendants of that cellular ancestor that had the great idea to bet on the strategy of code translation. Among all those who tried their hand at life, we have just one universal ancestor. At the moment it exploded, life became inventive, improvising different forms and techniques. Bacteria, plants, animals, humans—all with the same ancestry, that is, the right one.

The strategy of the victors was the strategy of cellular life, of code translation. The same code for everyone to translate to make it work. The same book, the same law for all life on Earth. Nature invented the cult of the Book millions of years before the first human writing. But a code is worthless if it isn't translated into the language of the living, and no virus can translate code into activity by itself. Viruses are clearly the losers in evolution, albeit losers who have assimilated the principle of the code for their survival. That is the power of the victor's law.

Viruses depend on cellular life and its translation skills to reproduce and ensure the survival of their own genetic code, and to be able to name it, to describe how the virus operates in the world of the living, Sadie must translate its code into proteins. She must become the translator of viral strategy in the language of the living.

XX

Sadie has temporarily joined Claire's lab, she's been given access codes. Everyone at the Hôtel-Dieu loves her father, which makes things easier. She tries not to think about it. People approach her sometimes, in the corridor, in the cafeteria, to express their sympathy about her mother, and also to get a glimpse of the prodigal daughter, how sad about Mrs. Dr. X, kindness incarnate, they say regretfully, such a lovely woman.

All day long, Claire and Sadie produce analyses. They cast the net wide. They copy the virus, make it multiply. In the middle of the lab where she coordinates the appetite and digestion of her behemoths, Claire runs the powerful computer programs. Sadie watches her move from one to the other, measuring their progression, anticipating the arrival of a new pile of results like the tamer of a gleaming horde. Once they have taken part in this kind of computer processing, many researchers and technicians begin to consider the virus as one moment among many others in the circulation of information they must decode. But Sadie notices the serious, almost solemn attention Claire pays to each transformation, from data to information, from information to knowledge. Claire explains to Sadie that she sees the passage of data through each machine, each program, each memory, as a moment of transformation of the code, as if the information were passing through different universes as it gets translated from one program to the other. She is the librarian of these universes.

X

Sadie walks back to her hotel at night, often late, crossing downtown from east to west. After all these years of walking through the winding streets of Marseille—narrow little roads like corridors hemmed in by stone walls that, depending on the time of day, absorb or exude heat—she has forgotten the incredible dimensions of North American cities. The contrast in scale is too great. She spends her days with her eyes glued either to the microscope, the vibration of amphorae, or trained on the series of capital letters in DNA sequences. When she emerges, her senses struggle to adjust to the monumental backdrop, immense glass walls soaring abruptly toward a violet sky that never seems to truly darken. Bright slices of skyscrapers interrupt the view with purple or blue or green neon, reminding Sadie of the gaudy red and yellow lights of the cabarets and casinos that once lit up the night sky, but these are sleeker, cleaner lines, meant to make people forget the bad taste of that early wealth. Downtown unfolds in a shimmering glow that dazzles her while the materiality of its surfaces slips away in a vanishing point that's impossible to locate.

Her body has been shaped by the crevices of ancient cities, the uneven surface of paving stones, she lives in a city of rough edges, a city that jolts her at every step, with the ridged seams that inhibit her stride. Here, her routes through the city are too smooth, her steps even and consistent, as steady as a timeless mantra, she slips on the false youth of this city of mirrors that never ceases to reflect back to her a misshapen silhouette.

Montreal is frozen over. The resurrection of spring has not yet arrived. In this foreign environment, she realizes the extent to which her body has nothing to do with Montreal anymore. Marseille awakened a certain genetic past in her that would have otherwise remained silent and left other aspects in a state of inertia they would not have known here. Genes that lay dormant in their sequence, and which had been reactivated by her migration. When she left to live on the other side of the ocean, the community of her genes carried her backward through American history, reconfigured her corporal envelope against the grain of that aberration. Her code was translated into a language that would no longer understand Montreal's code.

The only hypothesis she has to explain this incredible proportion of genes that code unknown proteins in the virus is that some ancestor, somewhere in the past, must have carried those genes, which the other members of the family have since jettisoned. Those genes speak a language that sounds incomprehensible to us because an ancient memory, lost along the road of evolution, has survived in them. That is what Régnier is determined to prove.

The only logical hypothesis.

She can hear him, as if on a loop, telling her about the lost ancestor and its slow degradation leading up to the contemporary virus. As she walks alone, she plays the role of Régnier in the conversation.

She reproduces the inflection with which he pretends to be sorry about this inevitability, then recovers with a half-smile. She thinks through the retort in the game where they each have their role to play. She knows his lines; in the deserted streets of downtown she recreates the little theatre of their conversations. Régnier's ideas do not emerge pure and intangible, they arise in the gestures that embody them, where they have their own way. She fleshes out Régnier's thought. She plays its detours, its rebounds, the rhetorical volume. She gives it back its style.

When an idea starts to bubble up in her, she needs to share it so that he can help her bring it to life. It only becomes an idea when she shares it. Sadie needs to off-load the movement, the impulse of thought so that, through contact with another thought, an idea can take shape.

There are moments when she burns to call Régnier or to send him the results. She urgently needs another set of eyes, another brain, other points of contact to reread what she is replaying again and again, in vain. She runs through the same numbers, the same diagrams. A stranger that can express itself in human language, but only to tell her how little she knows about it. This incomprehension arouses a variety of actions and reactions in her, but she can't make sense of anything. Something's wrong, she can't see where the unknown genes are coming from. Her mind needs to rub up against another to kick into gear.

The explanation can only come from above, Sadie.
Sometime in the past, an even more giant, more complex
ancestor existed, and these viruses are the degraded

descendants of that ancestor. We can't create something from
nothing, Sadie. We can't create something bigger from
something smaller.

The incomprehensible song of the virus plays on repeat in her head, with Régnier's refrain responding. Between the two echoes her need to make sense of it. Sadie goes in circles, always coming back to the same point, replaying the same scene. The unknown activates something in her, but she doesn't have what it would take to move forward, she's spinning her wheels, so she needs another voice, another reading to get her out of this impasse, but before she even acts on the impulse, she knows the response she'll receive, Régnier's mind has reached a dead end, which forces both of them to look back, we don't create something out of nothing, Sadie.

There's no other possible explanation, Sadie, the inflection of feigned regret, then the little smile, the table is laid, the sets are ready, the actors' marks have been placed on stage. Throughout the theorizing performance, she continuously plays and replays every gesture that reaches toward an explanation of the virus's code. But she can wreck her eyes and rack her brain all she wants—she can't see anything. Sometimes, she has the dizzy feeling of those dreams where she's suddenly forced to appear onstage, to recite lines she forgets instantly, or which she forgot to learn. She definitely remembers—a false memory, a dreamworld trompe l'oeil—that she was given the script, she accepted the role, but everything since has been erased and now they're all waiting for her on stage.

She can't see anything, all she can do is reread the text of the virus, go back over the data sequence. She knows that, logically, she won't find anything the computer hasn't already spotted, but since she has nothing else to do, she keeps generating analyses, going over them again and again, generating more analyses, putting the genome of the virus through the sieve of an ever-finer grid, again and again, compare, compare, compare.

XX

Genetic comparison between members of the same family—this is how the data is supposed to be organized. Usually, with each new specimen that joins the family, the understanding of the whole is further refined. The more expansive the knowledge, the more precise the detail. As Sadie compares the data from the new virus with the data from *Pandoravirus salinus, Pandoravirus dulcis, Pandoravirus quercus,* and *Pandoravirus inopinatum,* she relies on that idea, in the shape of an amphora, that name, Pandora, because in order to consider the differences and the relationships, she needs the concept of family, that common measure that allows her to hold them all together as a whole.

We're opening a Pandora's box, Sadie.

Régnier had established the notion of a whole that would be the basis for all the rest to come, the unknowns that had yet to appear before them, and he knew what he was doing. He had not just named the virus fished out of the sediments off the coast of Chile, not just named the moment when, under the microscope, the specimen revealed its alterity. He had named the joy of naming his own conceptual construction, which from that moment on would constitute the common measure of their research for the coming years, he was signing it for posterity. Everything that would come after would be identified as Pandora, he was already condensing every specificity, every difference, every variation into this name, all the potential novelty that the future was brimming with was all already contained in that generic idea. The future of the virus would only be thinkable in reference to the family name, a nomenclature that already held all potentialities, saved from dispersion in the name of Pandora.

The practice of scientific thought is bound up in the comparative method. The unexpected can only be thought of in relation to the idea of a whole, whether it's a family of viruses or the big family to which we believe all the different forms of life on Earth belong. You're either part of the family, or you're not.

That's the method, and it's not Sadie's place to break with it. The name calls her back to the exercise of comparison, calls upon her to pose as a third party, an intelligence capable of holding different concepts in her mind, one virus and another, in order to establish their relationships. She has only those methodological tools to use on the virus.

When she finally writes to Régnier, she'll have to send him a report, the data they've collected, and for that she will have to come up with a name, or rather, a specific epithet, that will identify this new branch of the virus. She already knows that Régnier will want to please her, and will propose *Pandoravirus montrealis*. To declare that this virus arose out of her return to Montreal. Declaring at the same time, for Sadie, that the city had remained the same. The genetic code changes as soon as a life, even an embryonic one, takes possession of it, but the name stays. The name persists in denying constant transformation. Sadie can't focus on the movements proliferating before her eyes, day after day, she can't bring herself to accept the name. On the forms at the lab, on the samples, in the growing piles of paperwork, she writes a simple X everywhere.

X

She and Claire are quickly growing closer, and Sadie is hesitant. With the exception of Régnier, she generally doesn't get too close to her colleagues. With Claire, things are getting more intense, there's no point in denying it, she recognizes the process, and when this happens, she just has to let it run its course, burst the abscess of desire in order to move on to something else.

But in this case, the situation is getting more complicated. She felt it from the start, but couldn't see it clearly, couldn't put it into words. She takes Claire's way of addressing her personally, and yet she also hears in it a call that goes through her, so to speak, and continues on toward something else, something that doesn't really have anything to do with her.

What is happening between them is created and evolves within their shared attention to the amphorae multiplying before their eyes, the development of speculative forms, the tension toward a vanishing point of knowledge. She can't see an end to it. A loop is being created between their overheating minds. A connection.

They are feeling their way through the same unknown, but they can't coexist within it, that unknown has different contours for each of them, it takes different shapes that are impossible to convey. Despite everything, the blindness of the pursuit creates a bond between them.

Claire is spending a lot of time on this project, and she's falling behind in her own work. Sadie knows she's distracting her from her usual tasks, that she's pulling her attention away from her daily life. But it's too late once they are swept up in this current. She is sucked in, Sadie takes her time, her attention, her imagination.

X X

When she gets back to the hotel at night, Sadie stops for a moment by the side entrance on Mansfield to smoke one of the joints Claire gave her, ordered online from the new government-owned cannabis corporation. They arrive neatly packaged in plastic and aluminum, sterile, inside a cardboard box that has a locking mechanism. The government seems to go to great lengths to make sure that even drugs create garbage. The package identifies the cannabis by variety, dominant hydrocarbons, and psychotropic content, letting people know what they're in for. Drug use has become pharmaceutical since the government started selling it. Now you can smoke in percentages, almost down to the milligram. There's no way to overdo it anymore. They'll get over it, Sadie thinks.

In a few decades, once it's become normal for the government to deal pot, the whole approach will be more stylized. The unpredictable will be sold according to popular trends, no longer identified by chemical substances, but instead sporting simplified designs, and colour-coded to facilitate gastronomic pairing. Altered states, if there is such a thing as a normal state, will be tailored to the leisure activities of their distinguished clients: for a night at the opera, we'll go with magenta, but if it's for dinner with the in-laws, better off with brown. There'll even be ads on the bus, urging people to abuse in moderation. This makes Sadie sad for the future of weed, but she hopes that by then the younger generations will have found new psychotropic landscapes to explore while their grandparents are carefully managing their cannabis pill organizers.

As her thoughts race, the air becomes crisper, and all the data that has accumulated in her mind throughout the day is redistributed into a new metabolism. She wouldn't be doing her job if she didn't allow her brain a little recreation, especially since that's where an essential part of her work takes place. It's the only way, or at least the most effective way, to allow the knowledge that piles up in her memory, all the measures and observations that add up throughout the day, to wander down otherwise inaccessible neuronal pathways. Those routes reinvent themselves, surprising her. Crossroads suddenly become highways, dead ends open up onto a megacity with a party in full swing.

Little will remain of these epiphanies tomorrow morning, but that's not the idea anyway. It's about getting off on revelation, again and again. The feeling of opening, expansion, when an idea emerges and broadens what was already there. It's never violent, it doesn't feel like a schism or a break. It distorts the world gracefully, it doesn't stop at the appearance of a skull and crossbones, the eureka moment never ends in that elastic time.

Start with the smallest things in existence and create something bigger.

Her only rule is to write nothing down. To retain nothing, even if her fingers are burning with it. Just get on the roller coaster and follow the hyperbole of thought. It's hard, she wants to take notes every time, she wants to write down every new hypothesis that emerges, leave a trace of the effervescence, pin down the invention. But that's not the idea of the high. Any record would be too firmly tied to the moment of its conception. A present already past. The idea of the high is stylistic, the truth it delivers will be of no use the next day.

The idea of the high emerges, changes everything around it, and the changed atmosphere produces another idea, which could never have existed without that alteration, the structure of thought is redeployed in a new way, it's a choreography that must be followed. There is a strong temptation to resist, to stop the machine to set down the skeleton on paper, but the only thing to do is to stay on the ride, slip into that metamorphic dance where thought is astonished anew each time, surprising itself in a new position.

Don't hold the position, listen to it, then let it waver, let it take us elsewhere.

That's the unexpected pleasure of the high, that moment of transference in which the idea escapes us, loses its consistency, and morphs into something else; we let go of what we were holding onto and what seemed to us so true, what had redefined, briefly, the categories of the real, what finally made us see differently.

That's the pleasure of melting into the translation of one moment to another, until the greatest intensity becomes the passage itself, the friction of time that turns the most recent past into antiquity.

The next day, nothing will be left but the joy of having seen.

to: asst.director@virolab-marseille.fr
from: director@virolab-marseille.fr

subject: ?

~~Sadie, dear Sadie~~

I hop everything is going well in montreal. I was wonderign when you can send me the analyses? i'll keep an eye on the intranet

It's been beautiful here lately really beautiful but I haven't been out much, you know how the changes in pressure are hard for me. I went back on the cortisone so we'll see.

Talk to you very soon

Im attaching my talk for next monday. Would you mind taking a look

Att. Dogmabusters_Dublin.docx

XX

"Dogma busters." This is one of Régnier's pet phrases when he lectures. He loves standing before a crowd of wide-eyed students and researchers and telling them how, on a boat off the coast of Chile, they had "opened a Pandora's box."

Pandora was sent by the gods to punish the unchecked ambition of humankind, who had stolen the fire of knowledge. Régnier enjoys making himself the artist of that supernatural punishment. He loves getting up in front of rows of attentive listeners to re-enact the drama of the humiliation of humanity, the appearance of these phenomena that confront us with the unknown, that make us question every method we'd had up until then to measure the world of the minuscule. He wields his diagrams and graphics, brandishing his weapon—desecration—and his army of iconoclasts. Puffed up with the pride of a general, he flaunts the photos of his troops in full infectious offensive.

It's a flawless performance. This is not the time to change tack. Régnier has no more tolerance for risk. Over the last few years, he and Sadie made the decision to allocate a significant proportion of their staff to the search for the ancestor of the giant viruses, the origin of all these unknown genes. The team could no longer afford to spread itself thin on useless working hypotheses. It was better to go all in on the most likely one, which subscribes to the dominant theory of evolutionary reduction. Régnier and Sadie have made it too far, their discovery, their precious amphora, has placed them in a very advantageous position, and now they can't risk discrediting themselves.

Régnier has been waiting a long time to watch everyone who looked down on him eat his dust. He banked his resentment throughout his whole career, and now, with the discovery of the giant viruses, he's finally starting to see some returns.

His style embraces nomenclature, makes the best of the categories at his disposal. Sadie admires the effect, as always, she recognizes the momentum, the flashes of wit, but, in the calm of her hotel room, she notices that she's not trembling, she doesn't feel that fear that usually twists her guts when he is going to speak. The fear that he won't be up to it, that he'll choke, that he won't manage to deliver the speech.

Sadie finishes reading Régnier's lecture and her brain falls silent, she notices the hum of the ventilation system, it's been so long since she's tuned in to that low level of ambient noise. For so long, she has been living among the viruses, the music in her headphones, between the volcanic atmosphere of Marseille and her travels all over the world, the turbulence of airplanes, the machinery of ships. She lives with her senses permanently plugged into some input, right up against the engine of perpetual movement.

X

If she leaves here, if she goes back to Régnier in Marseille, she will have to repatriate her virus, which they will then integrate into the well-oiled machine of knowledge. And the machine will find a solution to its puzzle, Sadie knows. The instruments used to identify the virus will eventually succeed in naming what they will make it possible to recognize. The instruments always end up making sense of the world. No matter how unprecedented their findings may be, the knowledge machine will digest them, assimilate them into its language.

As Sadie reads Régnier's elegant sentences and turns of phrase, she can already see the virus finding its place. In her turmoil, her incurable uncertainty, she clung to this brilliance, the intelligence of the world to which she had contributed. Because she recognized in it the incredible energy of a loser, the arrogance of an ambitious decadent, the distinction of a motivated paranoiac. Thrashing about together on a raft against the tide of the world.

In the text she has before her, she can imagine Régnier pacing the stage, expertly wielding his jittery nervousness, she can see the little bombshells coming. His thinking has become stylized, but along the way that style has hardened, congealed. She can't quite see where the virus could slip in there, how it could still have anything to teach him.

Régnier thinks in terms of winners and losers. He found the formula for success, and in his own thinking he left behind his loser status. He has become a system.

What they could learn from the virus, once she brings it back, once she introduces it into the system, will be nothing more than a question of rebranding.

XX

One evening, as they are wrapping up in the lab, Claire invites her to go out dancing. Sadie wonders where people go dancing in Montreal these days, the bars she's seen on Saint-Laurent with their long lineups of heavily made-up girls shivering in the cold are not too appealing. Claire says you just have to know where to look. They leave the hospital and stop at Place d'Armes, on the steps of the Notre-Dame Basilica, so Claire can roll a joint.

"There aren't a ton of queer bars in Montreal," she says. Sadie takes this as a sign that Claire recognizes herself in that twenty-first century queerness, that she identifies with it, as those of her generation say.

"The lesbians never manage to make a real permanent space for themselves," she continues. She says that in her twenties, she often went dancing at Hydra, a lesbian bar near where she lives in Mile End. But the bar closed when the landlords wanted to triple the rent. "The lease wasn't renewed, and the space sat empty for years. Now it's a fried chicken chain. Montreal doesn't know how to

178

learn from its sister cities. It could borrow an idea or two from Berlin, or Dakar, or Barcelona. The kind of places that have resisted becoming megacities. When Hydra closed, nobody even fought for it. Or for Café Engels on the next block, killed by the same developers. And now the neighbourhood has started converting triplexes into two-million-dollar villas. Young millionaires don't want to live in the suburbs anymore, or in the museums of upper Outremont. They want a 'real neighbourhood,' a 'community,' but to them community means a wide variety of vegan restaurants. When I first moved to Mile End, it was a bit sketchy, the buildings were all shabby and pretty, and stuff would pile up out front, half garbage, half art. The old-style places started falling into disrepair, the ground torn up here and there, bricks crumbling into dust. I'm lucky to have been in the same apartment for fifteen years, and it's cheap. But the building is for sale. I have no idea what the guy on the third floor will do then, he's this eccentric musician who's barely functional. In Berlin, even in Kreuzberg, where the bougie types have long since taken over, there are collectives constantly graffitiing new buildings, they're determined to knock down the real estate values in the neighbourhood, send the developers a message that they better hang on to their pressure washers if they want to make any money out of the place."

Claire is speaking faster and faster and then, getting up, puffs on the joint she's lit. "Anyway, the new queer generation isn't interested in property anymore, they're more into pop-up events."

Sadie still can't quite situate Claire with respect to that generation. She seemed to be among them, but now she's talking like they've passed her by, at least in part. Sometimes her expression seems hopeful, or enthusiastic, like she wants to adapt to the fluidity of her time. She has one foot in the community. She pronounces certain names as if she's evoking a collection of precious gems to show Sadie later. But Sadie also senses that it's all moving a bit too fast for Claire, that the past is holding onto her as she tries to catch a train that left a little too early.

Earlier, someone had texted Claire the address of a warehouse where a movie is being shot, an independent film about a vampire apocalypse. A friend of Claire's is the DOP, and tonight they're filming a big nightclub scene. "They need a lot of extras for the background. They'll provide the drinks, the teeth, and the contact lenses."

At ten, they start walking toward a neighbourhood in the north of the city that Sadie has only ever known as an industrial enclave. On Saint-Laurent, they hop on the bus that crosses the island from south to north. They get off in Little Italy and head west. At first, the area is still the no man's land that Sadie remembers. But then Claire leads her along a sinuous route, left and then right, down streets that come to abrupt dead ends, cutting across parking lots and abandoned lots to hit another road that comes out of nowhere. Old factories a few stories high sit alongside small blocks of residential duplexes in a way that betrays a lack of any particular urban planning. Claire knows where she's going, barely looking up as she walks. Sadie lets herself be carried along, the effect of the drugs contributing to the erratic feeling of their route, and it feels good to just be along for the ride. Claire carves out narrow passages in the déjà vu of the city, time regains a certain density.

Heavy bass notes can be heard in the distance. They're almost there. They reach a drab building with no sign or distinguishing features and go around the side to a loading zone, where a small crowd of people are gathering in colourful interpretations of futuristic vampires. Claire recognizes nobody and leads Sadie into the mass of creatures with white eyes.

X

Nobody warned them that there wouldn't be music. When they shout "Action!" bodies start to move nonchalantly. The stark lighting lacks nuance, the strobe lights create an exaggerated ambiance, forcing the jerky apparition of powdered faces nervously but discreetly tracking the camera. The actors enter. Sadie doesn't know much about the script, a makeup artist told her something about a complicated love story between two vampires just before the end of the world. The couple moves toward the middle of the dance floor, they're going to dance together, it's the scene where they first meet. The two actors approach one another. Their love awaits them. Alone in the darkness, two pale faces emerge. Their complexions are supposed to signify their tragic immortality, but the makeup is a bit too thick, like bad death masks. Sadie's not supposed to look at them, the only instruction the extras got was to not look at the actors, to act as if nothing was going on. Cut. They cut several times, the scene isn't working. Someone convinces the director to put on music to help with the atmosphere, but the music doesn't fit, the DJ is another actor and he puts on a track by Robyn to energize the crowd. While in other circumstances the Swedish pop star's dance-cry might work, Sadie feels like it's falling flat here, the scene is just not holding together. The dancers are distracted, the bass can't fill the room. The transition from one track to the next only calls attention to the interruption. Nothing inside Sadie can relax. She misses Molly, misses her artful metamorphoses. Sadie calls up Molly's movements inside herself, her rigid, metallic undulations. When she manages to reproduce those angles, the space around her starts to feel less hostile.

At some point, Sadie lost sight of the couple, and then suddenly the actor's caked-up face appears right beside her, so close she has the awkward feeling he might even want to dance with her. His face looks different up close, what from afar was a powdery pallor has taken on a viscous consistency with his sweat, his white face now shiny and glossy. She can't help but be touched by his beauty. Sadie doesn't know how he can be hot enough to sweat, the room is drafty, letting in the sharp air from outside, she's shivering even as she dances. He needs his makeup retouched, they are almost definitely going to cut any moment now. That'll be her chance to leave, she just has to find Claire to tell her she's had enough. Sadie looks for the other face in the crowd, the actress, but the vampire finds the girl first, he embraces his beloved in a gesture that doesn't manage to be quite brutal enough, it won't succeed in signifying peril onscreen. He is straining toward an expression of his love, but the fibres pull apart with the effort and threaten to scatter around the room, unable to signal anything. He mustn't know the brutality of love, or at least his body doesn't have the language for it, he could summon up everything inside him and still not transcend the limits of interpretation. There's a violence inside him that he's unaware of and Sadie would like to seek it out in the depths of his guts, she doesn't know why exactly, but she is taking his incompetence personally. She can't tear herself away from the pitiful performance, she would like him to find the strength of his unhappiness within himself, she would like for him to finally be able to summon the courage to accept the violence that could break through the reassuring mediocrity of his game, bring him to a breaking point.

She wants to believe that he could get there, that he has it in him. She wants him to be able to recognize the brutality he carries within him, let it twist and contort his features. She wants something to break up the sterile scene. She looks around for Claire's face, but finds only the counterfeit gaze of the pale blue contact lenses, reverberating through the room. Nothing but eyes surrounding her, eyes open onto the void, fluorescent opaline faces. Nothing is happening among all these bodies, nothing is being communicated. She is alone in the crowd of extras, the bad blood circulating in her can't find a way in, just rebounds off their reflective surface, it starts again, it's no longer a numbness but now more like a detachment, from the walls of her being—is she still dancing? She looks at her arms and her hands, not sure what connects them to her, if she is the one moving them—her feeling of selfhood is reduced to her eyes, she can feel them bulging, she must really have the face of a vampire in her final round, she must be the only one actually playing her part in this apocalypse, it seems very unlikely that she still has the use of her arms, they must be just hanging there miserably, and now her head too seems to be bent a little, like a sad Christ, she lets the image wash over her, she doesn't have enough control over her will to ward off something so ridiculous, a disjointed Christ slumping on his cross, without a Mater Dolorosa to mourn her, to collect what is leaking out of her, fluid but slow, she is missing many limbs, the horizontal and the vertical no longer hold in the axis, her neck will eventually give way, her heavy head leaning forward still, she's going to lose it this time—there's nothing in her now but the pain that pulses, breathes, she has only this pain to come back to the world.

She doesn't know how to collect herself to start looking for Claire again, but she wants her near, she wants Claire to pull her out of this state. She can't see Claire, but spots the lead actress, who seems so tired, like she wants to sleep for a century, the night scene is too much for her, she wants to quit, the film is clearly going to suck, but her contract prevents her from fleeing before her lover breaks the news about her immortality, so she's stuck here for eternity, she should have gone to med school when there was still time, she had potential, she had the discipline, she was always praised for her sound judgment, after every flop she told herself okay, I'll go back, and then she went and fell in love with another mediocre actor, and now here she is, stuck in this unending night, when are they going to cut, the scene isn't working, it's obvious, the actor's face is collapsing, the end of the world is promised to everyone except her...

"Sadie!" She recognizes the voice. Someone takes her hand and soon she's outside, the fresh air rushing into her lungs, it burns, reviving her a little from the inside. It must be very late, Sadie feels like they were in that bad movie for hours, but Claire sets her straight, a half hour, max.

"It sucks here. Trix just texted me, there's a Red Roam night in the basement of a place that used to be an old folks' home."

X

Trix is one of the names that Claire speaks with particular emotion, giving it a precious shine. Sadie follows Claire into an Uber, and they speed through the city. She doesn't try to figure out where they're going, she has her head turned to Claire, who hasn't let go of her hand. When she remembers to look out the window, the car is on the highway, heading out of the city, and then, a few minutes later, back into it through a different neighbourhood. With this fragmented version of Montreal, Claire lets her see flashes of its present tense, a city that is more than just déjà vu.

When they get out of the car, Sadie doesn't recognize anything, the street lined with two-storey buildings is quiet. Claire tells her they're in the southwest, and she stops in front of a dilapidated building with a sign screwed into the brown brick that reads, "Symbiosis Golden Age Home." Claire looks at her phone and heads toward the side of the building, to a heavy metal door that opens onto a set of stairs going down. The bass takes Sadie by storm, and the electric guitar doubles the bass, by the time Sadie and Claire reach a second door to the basement, the music is nothing but a beat that cuts right through them. Sadie suddenly has no idea what she's doing there, she doesn't know what it is in

Claire that she's following, but she doesn't investigate any further, she dives into the room with her.

The air suddenly becomes thick and rich with an indistinguishable alloy of humidity, smells, sound. The density of the space has a gravitational pull that sucks her in, she just has to slide into what's already there. Claire is holding her hand, and Sadie wonders if she's been holding it since the warehouse. The dancers are unaware of their presence, they can melt into what has already been built, what has been building for hours. Claire doesn't stop, she pushes deeper and deeper into the room. They are already dancing when Sadie picks the thread back up, the evening unravelling like frayed cloth. They don't look at each other as they dance, instead they keep finding a new space, they respond to the bass, the synthetic textures of the sound, perpetuating the rhythm that envelopes them. Sadie comes back to Claire's face, it is Claire who has made this place exist, a pocket where she can finally breathe.

She sees the same faces and hands again and again and they become familiar. A sense of redundancy is created. A girl suddenly emerges out of the blur. She has an actor's timing, straight black hair puffed up in a bouffant like a starlet from another era. Her face, pale and almost suspiciously symmetrical, is covered in rice powder. Fake nails painted black and white. This must be Trix. She's wearing a metallic belt over her hips, she starts to move and the golden discs hanging from the belt begin to move too, clinking together. Sadie's eyes are riveted on the little coins tinkling around her hips. She doesn't need to look around to know that other gazes are fixed on the glittering. Claire too. That's why she's here. The sound unfurls like a corridor for Trix's performance, and here in the basement of the Symbiosis, the electric chords unleash their very first reverberations, transmitting a little shock to Sadie, who immediately recognizes the riff, it's "Yaz Gazeteci Yaz," Selda Bağcan's powerful litany is channeled through Trix's body, liquid garnet running down her spine.

Sadie saw the Turkish singer in concert a few years earlier. Molly had convinced her to take a few days off and come to a Jewish music festival in Kraków. It was Selda Molly wanted to see, she was fascinated by the woman who'd been pissing off the conservative Turkish regime with her electric guitar since the seventies. She'd been imprisoned and persecuted, her songs had been banned, and she'd ended up becoming an international legend. In the middle of August, Molly dragged Sadie around in Kraków's humid heat, straight into the heart of the old Jewish quarter, still more or less untouched, where a crowd was gathering to hear the music that had once lived inside these walls, music that came from this place, from these Jewish enclaves in the heart of Europe. When Selda took the stage, late in the evening, accompanied by a group of young, slightly hipster musicians from Tel Aviv, Sadie's first impression was of an old granny in a floral blouse and perm, waving to the crowd like a matriarch arriving at Sunday dinner. When the first electric notes of "Yaz Gazeteci Yaz" rang out, when the small woman stepped up to the microphone and released her powerful invocation with a single breath, Sadie realized this wasn't any old flowery grandma. She already knew the song, she knew the voice from nearly every one of Molly's mixes, but associating that voice with this contingent human figure that was giving off an almost supernatural strength, standing before these young musicians carried by her boundless current, it was like time had twisted back on itself. Her voice may have thickened a little since the recordings in the seventies, but her exhortation to journalists to tell the truth resonated through the ages.

Sadie has not taken her eyes off the movement of the little metal discs. Right next to her, Claire too is gravitating in Trix's orbit. It's not only her body that is so compelling, it's an energy that precedes the body. Sadie can feel the full force of her fascination with Trix's dancing form strike her before it focuses into desire. The magnetic attraction emanating from her pulls in everyone around her, and Sadie feels herself joining an irreducible multitude of desires. She barely has time to notice Trix's attention narrowing in on her before heat spreads along her spine.

"Nice fangs."

Sadie realizes that she still has her vampire canines stuck to her teeth. She starts sweating. Trix hugs Claire and suggests they go smoke outside. Sadie agrees, and they follow Trix, who parts the crowd on her way. Outside, Trix pulls out a silver case and offers Claire and then Sadie a cigarette. To Sadie, she says, in English, "Claire tells me you're also an exile from philosophy?"

"Oh no, well, yes, in a way. And you?" Sadie says.

"I did my PhD in the States. On Spinoza. Can you fucking believe it? I wanted to be a college professor, the whole shebang. But I just loved sequins and fake lashes too much."

"She's becoming a YouTube star instead," says Claire, stretching out her neck as if to bring her face closer to Trix's.

"Oh please, gorge, I was born a star. It just took some time for the world to catch up," she says, sarcastic.

Trix's hammy maverick act breaks down into a cleverly disarming smile, a shift that reveals the complex coexistence of megalomania and self-deprecation.

"Seriously, though, I didn't plan to, like, work on YouTube, whatever that means. But I didn't plan to transition either, so there's that."

"Her alter ego, AmbienValence, is a contemporary Socrates," Claire explains, her eyes still on Trix. Sadie recognizes the attention, this move of Claire's, Trix on the receiving end of it now. "Socrates with way too much style, let's say," Trix adds. "But yeah, I guess it's still about sex, drugs, and politics. Trying to bring a little irony to the platform. But honestly, living online, it's super fucking exhausting. I can't keep up with *The Young and the Restless*."

Sadie thinks that Trix looks anything but exhausted. Sadie questions her. Trix elaborates. She isn't fully engaged in the grueling race. She dips her words in the current of contemporary culture, but doesn't stay there. Sadie can't quite locate what era Trix belongs to, Trix who protects her precious timelessness while still allowing herself to be contaminated in moderation, altered in measured proportions by the current moment. Sadie doesn't ask about the past, even a dinosaur like her knows the difference of that. Even if she knew more about Trix's life before, about her evolution, it wouldn't solve the mystery. Beneath the dazzling performance of self, her silence contains, somewhere, the possibility of a reversal of fate.

"I'm making a living off views now. It's still insane to me. When I started, I was a depressed and confused twenty-seven-year-old guy who had just moved back home after dropping out of grad school. I was making videos from my sad little room."

Sadie watches Trix, trying to decipher the details of her mannerisms. She also watches Claire watching Trix with an almost painfully tense smile. Claire's love is obvious. Sadie can see the blind, destructive force of passion in Claire, the desire eating away at a barricade, a dam inside her. Sadie is captivated by Trix's powerful individuality; listening to her speak, she can feel her own boundaries start to blur. She is also Claire watching Trix, she is the hundreds, the hundreds of thousands, who know Trix, who watch her. The air feels less harsh outside now, less brutal, something new is circulating, time becoming entangled in a sticky inner heat.

Trix continues in a hesitant Frenglish: "I left the bubble of the university, and all I did was watch videos all day. C'est le temps que YouTube a changé l'algorithm, it was to try to get people to stay on the platform for longer times. It was suggesting the weirdest shit to me, more and more extreme political stuff, more and more right wing. Je ne savais pas, there was this whole parallel universe, I was discovering a whole world. I really went down the rabbit hole, and honey, it was nauseating. Mes premiers vidéos, they're just, like, responses to these extreme views. Et puis, un jour, I'm noticing, there are people watching. De plus en plus." She switches back to English. "So I guess I started to care more. And now, I pay the rent with views."

"Trix transitioned live on the internet," Claire says.

"Yeah...I made those old videos private though. They're still there, but kind of painful to watch now."

Claire and Sadie fall silent.

"My god, your faces!" Trix continues, laughing. "It's not so much the pre-transition me that's hard to see. It's seeing myself *as a self*. Now, when I see myself on videos, it's AmbienValence. It's costumes! Psychotropics! Visual effects! Plastics!"

X

When Sadie gets back to the hotel, it's almost daylight. She opens her computer and types "AmbienValence" in the search engine. She finds Trix's page, watches one video, then another. She adds her fascination to the astronomical number of views. AmbienValence's appearances are manifold, she makes every facet shine, she has an obvious gift for editing. She creates an aura of detachment only to suddenly break through it with intense bursts of affect.

The whole thing is executed with a magnificent sense of irony, but the real stroke of genius lies elsewhere. In moments, she lets the audience guess at the weak spots in the glossy surface, the places where her mask could crack and allow her to be dragged down in the net of a derisory authenticity.

Sadie sees something of Molly in Trix. They're the same age, both caught between two generations. Trix survived adolescence thanks to her fascination for the gay kitschification of the world, but she reached adulthood only to be spit out into a drastically literal moment. She is torn between two eras, and resisting in the gap. That's where she differs from Molly, who will defend her irrelevance to the point of decadence, to the point of tragedy. Trix earns her living through clicks and so she doesn't have the same freedom, she must tactfully manage her audience's thirst for identification.

Sadie can see what made Trix renounce academia to become another kind of teacher. Trix delivers her message through aesthetics, leaving behind the disillusioned and sedate, albeit purist, thinking of the classroom to make a spectacle of theory. That was how philosophy had seduced her in the first place—the performance of the serious. She must have made the mistake of underestimating the humourlessness of academics. Her current audience is just as weary, just as disillusioned, but in the darkest hours of their insomniac nights, they're listening. From one video to the next, their torpor sharpens into a slightly more alert attention, the content Trix pours into the bluish glow of their phones reaches more deeply into their neurons. AmbienValence articulates her ideas through costume changes, dissects nuance with the sharp tip of a fake nail. She makes her way through perilous spaces of thought, working without a net above the comment section, she wields the neologisms of contemporary extremes in a mash-up with the abstract concepts of her former life. She hasn't disavowed her education, she's found a new landscape in which to transplant the theories she's incorporated, she crossbreeds them, nurtures the growth of new species. Her followers, along with new viewers the algorithm spits out onto her page, sit up a little straighter, their brains perk up to follow along as Trix dismantles a syllogism, they relearn how to concentrate for longer than the duration of a TikTok video. But what strikes Sadie the most is the way Trix portrays the dissonance crystallized by paradoxes, making her unwilling persona face the subtle contradictions that everyone would prefer to just smooth away.

Sadie falls asleep to Trix's voice with the morning well underway. She dreams of thousands, millions of views, and then the numbers are transformed from abstractions into a profusion of limbs, countless tentacles that feel and taste, she herself is one of those living numbers, she can still feel Trix's presence, a voice that continues to speak through the computer and intrude into her sleeping brain, filtered through sleep, transformed by the different machines of the dream. Is Trix the sum of all these limbs? Her voice contains them, carries them, Sadie rests in it, she reaches out to touch the walls as if she were inside a giant fish, she moves among all the views swarming around her, the voice of Ambien-Valence still seeping into her consciousness, and as Trix shows another angle, the dream shifts its relationship to image, playing with the logic of what it is to see, Sadie's gaze becomes more and more tactile, the dream says no more than that, this gaze that becomes material, that gropes at the inner walls of that voice...

The significance of the dream is connected to her surroundings, she is no longer a being that touches, she is no longer even a mere limb as she is swept up in the current, swallowed up by a flood, a mix of views and visions convey their hunger and multiply, AmbienValence's voice speaks to her, but does not call her by her own name, she gurgles with more and more views that create a chaos of *click-click-click*, the belly of the fish will soon be full, the little fish will grow larger and larger, it reaches her throat, the seaweed wraps around her and the voice keeps coming through, calling more than she can hope to contain...

Soon, the images will have taken a turn that Sadie will not be able to explain upon waking, a less figurative texture, of which real life would have kept no trace if it weren't for the ringing telephone that pulls her abruptly into her waking consciousness by short-circuiting the normal progression of waking and doesn't leave her enough time to forget the strange sensation—an incoming call from her father—and in the rushed crossing of psychic layers, she remains under the influence of an experience without image, without shape or colour, a completely abstract experience—touch the green dot on the phone—a completely dark abstraction, except for the cacophony unbearable to her senses—"Hello, Sadie? We wanted to invite you to dinner tonight"—like the shrieking of an orchestra when the instruments are warming up in the pit, the moment of clamour that undoes the sound before the piece has even begun, on the edge of that abyss she hears herself say—"Yes, okay"—with the lingering aftertaste of having been no one at all.

to: asst.director@virolab-marseille.fr
from: director@virolab-marseille.fr
subject:

dear dear Sadir,

is there a problem maybe

i can see that you're connecting to the infranet, but i can't see
any results. is everything okay? did you find anything?

Everything is fine here, i am getting by even with the migraines
and spring, you know how transitions are hard for me,

but at the lab it's a bit tense, they're starting to freak out
without you.

Sadie are you freakign out too? I'm starting to stress a bit, if
something's up just write me at least.

take care of yourself, be careful to not wear yourself otuo

be safe, talk to you bery soon,

FR

oh did you have a change to look at my lecture?
i'll attach it again

Att. Dogmabreakers_Dublin.docx

XX

Sadie's father invited two of Sadie's sisters, the youngest, Françoise, and Marie, "to join us," he said, because we are, after all, a family.

At dusk, Sadie walks toward the house on Querbes, taking deep breaths of cold air that freezes her throat and lungs. She struggled to emerge from her dream, spending the whole afternoon in its grip, and yet was still unable to understand the experience. She could easily have stayed in the shower, scrubbing her skin forever, she hadn't managed to purge the night from the deepest layers. Like a scuba diver who surfaced too quickly, she feels like she witnessed psychic content that the normal mechanisms of her consciousness should have protected her from.

She's there. She rings the doorbell, and when her father opens the door, she's sucked inside by warm, fragrant air. She has never seen her father cook before. He takes her coat, explaining that he's been taking classes since he cut down on his work hours. Perhaps he missed cutting meat. He's wearing an apron from the Culinary Institute. He tells Sadie and her mother to go sit in the living room, he has to check on dinner. Clearly, with her father in the kitchen, weeknight cooking has been elevated to gastronomic art. Everything he touches becomes a serious undertaking.

Sadie stays in the living room with her mother, who maintains a reserve familiar to Sadie, but this time focused on a motive she can't manage to keep to herself. Sadie watches her mother work to summon up a friendly, affable air despite the nagging question: who exactly is this woman they've invited to dinner?

The sisters arrive together. They talk a lot and say very little. They have not maintained their relationship over the years. The banality of their conversation, the way they address their mother, it all covers up the obvious: how did they let this happen? But Sadie is the one who deserted them, so she has no say in the matter. She just keeps quiet and offers contextually appropriate courtesies. The conversation shifts awkwardly to the subject of the children, the nephews Sadie knows nothing about. She tries to match her facial expression to the interest she is feigning without much enthusiasm, but which seems to be the minimum human decency called for by the situation. Marie doesn't just look sad, she looks like something is broken inside her. Sadie recognizes her broad shoulders, she was athletic when she was young, her muscles still visible through her leggings. Sadie listens to her talk about her children, two young men who are clearly, despite their mother's encouraging remarks, a source of constant worry and disappointment. Françoise is small, compact, and nervous. Her anxiety unsettles the air. She's upset because her father wouldn't let her bring her dogs. "Two Newfoundland dogs," Marie explains, playing moderator.

While Françoise, who intends to cause trouble, refuses to drop the subject of her irritation, Sadie observes the relationships that have lasted. She watches these people struggling in the too-small garments of their own sadness. Her mother, sitting next to her daughters, looks reasonably good, sitting up straight in her chair. That look she used to have, like she was the guardian of the end of the world, has faded.

Eventually, Marie can't hold it in anymore, she turns to Sadie: "She was getting out. We couldn't manage anymore."

Her words hang there, a surplus of speech that nobody else picks up. Their father comes in to pour the wine. He serves his daughters, then his wife. The whole scene is only slightly out of sync. The house soon fills with the aroma of meat and sauces. Marie compliments their father. Françoise settles deeper into her scowl. Returning to this scene is nauseating. Sadie works hard to prevent the familial failure from clinging to her skin. She tries to play the observer, she might almost laugh about it if the others weren't determined to be so serious. They believe they're at the centre of a great tragedy, called upon to face the disaster of their fate. Reverence for their father is too much to ask of her, when the sketch so poorly covers up their contempt. She is willing to play the role, but would at least like a decent script, a somewhat coherent story.

Everyone is seated in their assigned places in the living room of the family home. Sadie keeps her arms crossed, her hands tight on her elbows, she tries hard to contain the feeling of a progressive blurring, her outline is vanishing. Most importantly, she must not give in to the empathy reflex. Do not build a bridge, do not put yourself in their shoes, stay put on the shore, safe on the banks alongside them. Keep an eye on the lines of communication. She concentrates on the image of an irrevocable chasm, an abyss she abruptly opened up by going off course, dynamiting the map that had been drawn out for her life. She wasn't the only one who left, there is a brother in the Florida swamps, a sister in the Prairies, in Manitoba. They visit sometimes, she's the only one with the courage to never come back. She left, she no longer belongs to this. She cleaved off, and when she focuses her mind on this image, this major redirection that's tearing apart the living room, she feels like she's regaining control. She thinks that her sister...no, it's her mother, look, it's all getting muddled up again, and her mother, in this upside-down logic, could also easily be her sister, and then her sisters, whose mother she was for all those years, with no recognition for the role, it all slips into, or rather marches through, Sadie's mind faster and faster, she feels herself warming up, starting to simmer like her father's little dishes, his great gastronomical creations, and it warms her like never before, no, really, what a cook, all the same, this is exactly what she wanted to avoid by forging an existence far from the family stew, by working to create a difference, otherwise, all sisters in that repressed hatred, they learned from the high priestess of calm, of morbid composure, her mother had mastered the art of sauces like nobody else and now that she has passed on her knowledge, she can rot serenely, she has turned her back on her pots and pans without a care for what is left behind, Sadie could almost find it beautiful, the late-in-life tranquility of that other sister.

They move to the table. Their father serves offal to start. Sadie hasn't eaten red meat in years. She tries not to think about it passing through her, viscera to viscera. She tries hard not to let herself be overwhelmed by the sight, the sound, the incessant movement of avid mouths greedily swallowing the stew. These people, who otherwise have such fine manners and so much consideration, gobble up the lamb stew served as a main course, barely closing their mouths, the sauce binding the fatty fiber of the muscles to their saliva, Sadie can't take her eyes off the slurry where mouth meets animal. Her family chats about mutual acquaintances and neighbourhood gossip before trivia branches out into politics. The most varied, miscellaneous facts are passed through the mill, an impressive quantity of topics piled up and pressed through the meat grinder of peremptory conversation. As long as they're busy destroying the outside world, they don't attack each other. Sadie's two sisters know the routine, they provide their father with reprehensible anecdotes, despicable characters, a variety of opportunities for irrefutable judgment. Sadie refrains. No, she will not participate in this discussion, she will not let herself be consumed by coercive forces that want to incorporate her into an elective "we" rolling around in her father's mouth. No. She holds back the objections that want to come out of her own mouth, even cutting the conversation off would be getting involved in it. No. She is no longer made of that same stuff. Sadie stays walled up, forcing herself to eat very slowly to drown out, with her own chewing, the wet noise of membranes, the smacking of tongues and mucosa. By the time they get up from the table, Sadie is exhausted. They retire to the living room for after-dinner drinks.

"So, dear, you were saying that you work..." Her mother comes back to life after having hung back during dinner, she addresses her daughter, letting her sentence trail off, waiting for this guest to finish it, leaving the missing information hanging as if it were only momentarily forgotten. Her mother's manners retain the strategies of reason, but they are distorted and destabilized by a new clumsiness. Her daughter, hypnotized by the dead air dragging on beyond the limits of the acceptable, finally answers: "In Marseille. I work in·a microbiology lab."

"Ah...One of our daughters lives in Marseille. She moved a long time ago. Maybe you know her? Her name is..."

Her mother doesn't finish her sentence. She doesn't know. Her face suddenly hardens. It's painful for her to have to speak of a difficult time in her life to a stranger. She didn't expect this guest to rekindle the irritation of the memory of that daughter.

Sadie looks at her sisters, who avoid her eyes, she looks at her father, she tries to figure out from his expression whether he intends to continue playing this game or whether he plans to bring this conversation back to reality at some point. Is he going to say it, the name, her name, in his French accent that makes it sound ridiculous, or is he going to leave the dirty job of breaking the spell to her, it would be a favour to everyone if Sadie would volunteer, take it upon herself.

Hi Mom, it's me, your ungrateful daughter, I'm back Mom. Dad whistled, so here I am, it's me, Sadie, the bad one, you remember, you're the one who came up with this name, you wanted it, it's you, that call, the future you gave me. See, all it took was a phone call and I came running back like a good little dog, Mom, I bet you never knew, you never really believed it either, but it turns out I'm actually a completely loyal daughter.

XX

She made a final attempt, a few years after leaving Montreal, she trampled on her own will, rode roughshod over herself to see what her mother would say. She had finished her PhD, and she looked back, for just a moment. She should have known it would never end well, wanting to save a mother so far gone, the walking dead. But she was suddenly struck with a wild energy that needed an immediate outlet.

It's stronger than her, that urge to seek a response when the fever overtakes her and demands to be shared, when it feels like the seams of her self are splitting. She can't handle the pressure. She needs it to find somewhere else to go. The friction will interrupt the centrifugal force, prevent it from spiralling until it spills out into the void.

She picked up the phone, her doctoral dissertation lying across her knees in a bulging pile. She was surprised to hear, for the first time, the transatlantic tone. Through a technical feat that suddenly seemed incredible to her, the two continents had been connected by cables that ran along the sea floor and would transmit her voice right into the heart of Montreal any second now. Her thoughts were tracing that underwater trajectory when she heard her mother's voice come over the line.

"Hello?"

"Mom? It's Sadie."

"Ah."

The single syllable already contained it all—the steely voice, the inflexible tone, the absence of any room for negotiation where maybe even a little warmth could have crept in. Before she even said a word, Sadie understood how stupid she'd been to imagine anything else. But there they were, so she'd have to say something.

"I finished my PhD..." As she wrenched the words from herself to try to make them stick to some maternal surface, Sadie saw the image of the successful daughter suddenly turn grotesque, an ungainly little mutt dragging home a stick all gnawed and dripping with slime, a ridiculous little creature panting at her own job well done.

"Well, dear. I don't really know why you felt you had to inform me."

There was a second of silence during which the pain spread, immobilizing her limbs, she hung up immediately so she wouldn't be heard. Her rage pinned her to the couch, she convulsed with it for some unknown span of time, writhing like the amputated stump of a human spit out into the world, before the anesthesia finally kicked in. What hurt so much was not the response, but that toneless voice she recognized with her flesh, in the response of her nerves, the tensing of her joints. What hurt was having opened up a space, a tiny little space, in which she had hoped to hear something different. She had let herself believe in a certain malleability, after all, she had succeeded in reinventing herself elsewhere, she had created another life for herself. She'd thought that, maybe, mathematically speaking, it might be a question of geometry, that the laws of dynamics would mean that something else had to be possible.

Alas, oh inflexible, steely voice. She wouldn't be caught again. That was her last relapse. Never again.

X X

After leaving her parents' house, Sadie walks through the frigid night. April is dragging on with no end in sight to the winter. Earlier in the evening, there was a hint of something gentler in the damp dusk. But now a few mocking snowflakes start to fall. Sadie's coat is too light and the wind freezes her bones and her leather boots soak up the brownish sludge of snow mixed with the pebbles and sand that the winter deposited, and which the new layer of snow will not manage to bleach out. Her spine is still locked and sends out shockwaves of pain, she forces herself to step lightly, she exaggerates the sway of her hips, tries to relax her muscles and ligaments against the brutal edge of the cold. Living through this, a never-ending winter, every year—this is what she escaped.

In Marseille, she might be swimming already. On Sunday afternoons she takes the bus on La Canebière along the Corniche seaside roadway and gets off at Malmousque, the old fishing port. When she wants something a little quieter, she rides two more stops and takes the steep, narrow streets to the Anse de la Fausse

Monnaie. She goes down the small stone steps and, as she passes beneath one of the arches of the old bridge, a small cove of big white rocks opens out onto the turquoise sea.

She avoids the big sandy beaches that are always packed on the weekends. Malmousque is livelier, mostly with families and kids playing noisily and throwing themselves into the water, but at Fausse Monnaie, everything is relaxed: people come to smoke joints, chat quietly, even the teenagers flirt at a different tempo, they're chill, they say things like, "Hey lady, God sure was good to you," and go back to their business. Comments like that haven't been directed at her in a few years now. She fades gently into the mountains. Small clusters of people occupy the rocks in mutual indifference, looking out at the sea that dominates the space. In the cove at Fausse Monnaie, the day is less tied to its hours, aligned instead with the transition of colour and light. The sea, which earlier shimmered with a beauty so vivid it was almost painful, drifts toward a pastel softness. The shades become velvety, the cove rests in the shadow of a luxury hotel patio that overlooks the water while shielding its guests from the public. The slope to reach the sea is slippery, the rocks covered with slimy algae and sharp shells. One summer she was caught by surprise, and struggled to climb back up as the waves swallowed her whole, one after another, the surf dragging her violently along the razor-edged shells, flaying her back, and then burning the open wounds with salt.

Veronica, Molly, and other friends often come meet her for drinks later in the day, but she likes to get there early to swim first. She swims with the horizon, and over the years has pinpointed the spot where she should turn around to be sure she has enough energy to make it back. There is always a vague fear subtly playing on her in the sustained exertion toward the open sea, an irrational fear at work in the movement of her muscles, that she could lose the pull of the coast, that she could drift away. Sometimes she pauses before swimming back to the white rocks in the distance, takes a few breaths, and lets herself float on her back, never for very long because to stay there, immobile, she has to forget the infinite number of living organisms flitting everywhere around her. She closes her eyes, stabilizes her body on the surface of the water, lets herself be carried by an invisible density, she never stays as long as she would like, a few seconds, long enough to forget the chasm stretching out beneath her.

The lights on Côte-Sainte-Catherine startle her back to the now freezing night. Walking into the wind toward the slope of the mountain that separates her from the city centre, she realizes she forgot her phone at her father's house. She turns back reluctantly, painfully retracing her steps despite the lamentations of her vertebrae. As she finally reaches the house, she is focused on the task at hand. The walkway is slippery, she puts a hand on the car to avoid falling on her ass and suddenly sees movement in her peripheral vision, something stirring close by, behind the frozen windshield of the car. Her brain is slow to register what's happening, and when she sticks her face up against the frost, her pulse accelerating, she makes out a mass of snarled hair, a naked form stirred by strange currents.

The body is thin and yet covered with so much skin, far too much skin floating around its bones. She can't compute how this could be her mother's body, she doesn't recognize this flaccidity.

She has never seen this before—and yet, the moment reminds her of something from the past, an image she can't quite make cohere into a precise memory.

She prepares herself to open the door, she is going to look past the staggering whiteness, and touch it. Sadie's stomach is roiling.

"Easy, mother. Easy. Let me take you home." She hears herself say this, she hears the voice coming out of her, attempting to reassure.

As she makes contact, the tension vanishes, the figure suddenly becomes quite flexible, conciliatory. She never had that flexibility. The matter that is her mother flows toward Sadie.

X

She took her mother in her arms, she lifted the featherlight weight of her mother's body, the body that for so long seemed so dense. In order to support the weight, Sadie's body regains a certain rigour. Adrenaline neutralizes her back pain, coursing through her bloodstream, activating the right reflexes. She carries her as a lover would, or a soulmate, or a mother, she carries her like a helpful, caring person would. She goes back into the silent house. A few lights are still on, a timer will switch off the lamps on the ground floor at ten o'clock. She hasn't gone upstairs since she's been back, she stayed on the ground floor, confined to the spaces reserved for guests. At the top of the stairs, she passes the bedroom where her father is already snoring, she walks to the end of the hallway, toward one of the children's rooms that her mother must now occupy.

She sets her down on the bed, her mother manages to sit up a little and Sadie moves quickly, opening two, three drawers of the massive dark wood dresser to find a nightgown that she then slips over her mother's head. She lays her mother down on the sheet and pulls up the quilt, tucking in the narrow shape of her body.

Sadie wants to leave immediately, but two eyes, wide open, keep her there. She stays sitting on the bed, and in the warmth of the covers, her mother's body starts to relax little by little.

There is no protocol for this kind of proximity. Sadie has no memory of this kind of close contact. She doesn't know what to do next, she doesn't know anything, her mother is vulnerable in a way she doesn't recognize, she doesn't know anything about it and she doesn't want to learn.

But her mother is still staring up at her, clinging to her with her eyes and not letting go. Of course, she's not looking at Sadie, she's appealing to the stranger in front of her who might be able to help her escape again, this stranger who could short-circuit the story, it's perfect, the traveller who has come to sever the thread of the too-familiar, this person who has no idea how things work around here, who introduces a continuity error, the person who, not knowing the customs, will poke a hole in the pattern. Yes, her mother could only open up like this, with this look, to this person who is nobody. But Sadie can no longer detach herself from the wordless gesture, her mother is now hanging onto Sadie's presence, if Sadie lets go, she will come undone, she might fall to pieces into the sheets. She wants Sadie to stay. That's what she wants. Sadie has never seen that kind of need in her mother's face, and yet her mother seems to have carried it inside her for a long time, she pulled out the expression from some distant place where perhaps she had waited a long time, staring at the vast expanses of sky, before someone came to pick her up, to take care of her. Waiting in the immense void for the world to suddenly make sense. Sadie's hands grow clammy, cold, and sticky as her fingers grasp at a distant memory.

Her mother is asking her to be everything, she believes she can be everything for her.

The whiteness that should overtake her, that should normally have already spread through her limbs, circulated through her bloodstream, frozen her lymph, calmed her innards, and muffled the racing of her heart, that whiteness has not set, it quivers like the albumen of a raw egg, the bright white of eyes glaring in the half-light, the white of milk, of gulping mouthfuls, of flowing mucus, of ravenous hunger. The woman before her can make anything possible, can do anything for her now. And that's what she wants from her, in that moment that is still raw, that won't set. Because Sadie can't quite get there, she can't become nobody. She has too many memories, too much has happened to halt the shocking collision of multiple streams of time, Sadie can't break away from the linearity of reading, and how shocking, this mother who doesn't know how to behave, who asks her for the future that lies before her, who wants to make her way in this new life that is beginning, who asks her for a tenderness that would allow her to believe in that new beginning. This woman who taught Sadie how to want nothing, how to expect nothing from life, is now a fount of boundless need.

PART 3

DE NOVO

She can't. She has to get out of here, right now, she has to leave, escape as soon as possible from a city that inevitably brings her back to the beginning of the story. The story refuses the march of progress, she should have known, or at least nurtured a healthy, rational doubt, after all, she has learned to side with doubt, a measured skepticism, yes, she is capable of doubt, she does it every day in her work, her observations of the world, she should have doubted that anything good could come of this.

She had been prepared to encounter the logical continuation of the past, she had calculated the state of it, in her most modest hypotheses, by adding the value "n" to represent the ongoing passage of time that had occurred in her absence. But in that ultra conservative estimate, she had not foreseen the appearance of a variable that follows no logic and refuses all continuity. She thought she was immunized against the pathology of memory, she hadn't expected—even though it's very true that she might have suspected—that the very logic of time would be affected, that she would arrive into a universe reinvented by senility, nothing good, absolutely nothing good, that much she had been prepared for. She knows how to protect herself against pathological agents, she could have isolated herself from them, but what she encountered in that bedroom and in that car was not something she could simply push away, and far worse than some horrible scene she might have encountered, which she could have contemplated with a revulsion that would be distressing but unable to really affect her, what had opened up before her tonight had looked back at her.

In that house, where every inch of space continues to preserve itself not just in her memory, but also in reality, persisting in the syrup of time to protect itself from any change, a voice calls to her, still inarticulate, a voice that delirium rediscovers and which asks her to hallucinate along with it.

See, Sadie, the room is not the same room of the past forever, come on, let's start all over again. Sadie, you're invited to an impossible equation, you're invited to rewrite the laws of time, maybe there is a way, in the senescence of forms, maybe there are other ways we didn't imagine.

Her thoughts spin and swirl, but cannot get past the vision of that nudity, the white flesh, the tumult of skin, even the hair she'd had to smooth back into place.

The ache in her back has shifted. Her lower back relaxed as the pain moved upward—from one disc to the next, her nerves passing on the message through the intravertebral foramen—all the way to her cervical spine. Sadie doesn't remember her neck ever hurting like this before, the pain detaches the tissues in her consciousness. She hasn't left her room in two days. The hotel bill must be astronomical, a major expense for the lab.

The primitive urge to flee came back stronger than ever that night at her parents' house. She rushed back to the hotel in a panic, okay let's go, just pack up and get out of here. She started furiously shoving things into her carry-on, as if there was much more to pack than the few clothes she'd brought along. But halfway through, a silk blouse in her hand, all the movement in her stopped short. Her neck and shoulders locked up and she was unable to make the next move. The cottony white was beginning to make its way through her, but as the familiar whiteness spread, something wavered. She couldn't reach the full oblivion that would finally wipe her system clean.

Her thoughts bounce off the wallpaper, amplified by the enclosed room, the sealed exits, even the giant window is more of a mirror than an opening. Her nerve endings sizzle, everything in her demands an answer. Call Régnier, explain everything, so he'll read it all again, the whole virus, from gene to gene, protein to protein, the whole unknowable mess, so he can send her another interpretation. But she can't manage the next gesture that will actually move her body in space. She keeps bouncing off the walls. If she walks out the door, she'll have to make a choice. In order to return to the world, she'll have to take the virus with her.

> *We can't create something bigger*
> *from something smaller, Sadie.*
> *The only possible explanation is genetic reduction.*
> *We can't create something bigger from something smaller.*

Régnier's words mingle with her own circuits. She can hear him, talking in the lab, giving a lecture, speaking at the conferences he's invited to. The evolution of life on Earth is under constant pressure, life is a struggle, only the victors survive. Life must be explained in vertical terms, there's no escape. There is no other way.

When Régnier arrives at an explanation, he keeps it on a short leash. There is great pressure in the world of scientific innovation, he must constantly watch his back, all those scumbags keeping an eye on him, ready to discredit him at the slightest misstep. A single study that can't be replicated, a hint of methodological trouble, and your career is destroyed. All the people who were so enthusiastic about your research, who hovered around your work waiting to snatch some little crumb for themselves, who until yesterday populated the small ecosystem that generates a promising field of experimentation. When your studies are successful, investors flock to you. But at the first glitch, the leeches bolt. They sever every tie, taking care to erase any trace of collaboration with the pariah du jour. Everyone everywhere busy editing their CVs, reformulating their research interests. For the last decade, Régnier has been featured on the cover of *Science Magazine*, he gets invited everywhere, he's won prizes. He can't afford to expose himself to the bastards who are just waiting for him to mess up so they can jump on his research grants. The closer you get to the top, the more expensive innovation becomes. Testing out a new theory means risking ending up in the gutter of posterity, without even a Wikipedia entry to record the mark you made on the world.

It's different for Sadie. She realized that at twenty-five, the day she attended a philosophy conference in Berlin, which was still opening back up to the world. The conference was being held in the main building of Humboldt-Universität, named for the father of modern universities. Entering from Unter den Linden into what first seemed more like a palace than a university, she solemnly climbed the imposing pink marble staircase. The names of those who'd worked within these walls replayed in her mind, G. W. F. Hegel, Arthur Schopenhauer, Walter Benjamin, Albert Einstein, Max Planck. The Faculty of Philosophy was still located in the main building, a reminder of a time when the natural sciences were dependent not on the Faculty of Medicine, but instead on the ultimate critical discipline. Upstairs, the walls of the main hall were lined with portraits. One stern-faced man after another, all with more or less the same expression. Trying to find her way, Sadie turned down a side corridor where she found portraits of a few women, most with Jewish names, mathematicians, physicists, chemists, who had been accepted as assistant professors starting in the early twentieth century, before the Nazis drove them out of the institution. History had quickly cast them aside, but their portraits, watching over these corridors of knowledge, remained.

Sadie recognized herself as a descendant of this lineup of losers. It was a certainty that took root in her. No matter how many firsts she accumulated, how many doors she opened, she would only ever end up with a portrait in a forgotten side corridor somewhere in the halls of knowledge.

Women are the losers who have always already lost the race. They must develop other tools, other strategies. Parasitize power. Learn the codes, learn to speak the language of the victors. Work from within the system, choosing the power of influence over the power of authority. Settle in the wings and let the boys up on stage kill each other for a place in the spotlight.

When she met Régnier, she suddenly had a few more resources at her disposal. He'd worked hard to secure his place in the institution, even though he despised everything institutional. The power of his contempt sustained his unquenchable thirst for recognition. Eccentric genius is a fraught position to defend. When he met Sadie, things became a little easier for him, he could rely on her patience, and especially on her skills in terms of personalities and dysfunctional systems. Once she got to work neutralizing any interference, any obstacles to his concentration, he could fully devote himself to what was important. It was unbelievable how much freedom her presence afforded him. He is sincere when he introduces her in his talks as the person "without whom, this work would not be possible." Régnier is grateful, after all.

Thinking back on that scene from Humboldt-Universität relaxes her. It always has that effect, Sadie thinks as she stares at the ceiling of her room, every time the pressure gets to be too much, it's restful to look at things from that perspective. She falls asleep with a renewed sense of her own limitations.

When she wakes up, she lies still for a long time in the big white bed, the wrinkled sheets, the fluffy undulations of the duvet. She didn't close the curtains before falling asleep and the direct light shining in on the bed creates the illusion that it is emanating from the white sheets, that it's the bed that's lighting up the room. The bed usually gets made daily, but now the bedding is all tangled. She'd like to have the room cleaned, to have someone come in and stretch the sheets tightly over the mattress as she herself is unable to do, she would like this to be taken care of for her, but that would mean leaving the room at least briefly, and she has no interest in going out into the common areas where she would have to exist among other people.

Her neck punishes her when she starts to move again, her muscles are still clenched, her shoulders, her collarbone, as if she's wearing armour that's trying to block the pain that wants to travel from her belly to her head. She can feel the fortress of her body struggle to resist the weakening; her mind, too, feels dull, less precise. She gets up painfully.

She has always envisioned her work in its final form, as if she were heading toward a goal, the attainment of the knowledge she works toward every day in the lab: her understanding of the virus. Sadie has trained herself in the constant tension of her expertise. Her process goes from data collection, to the intertwining of information, to the moment when it clicks and she can finally see. Her job is to learn.

She hasn't been back to Claire's lab in days. She's never spent this much time away from the microscope before. Even on research trips, even out in the middle of the sea, they recreate a little technical environment in some small space on the boats. The confinement of the lab, its white walls and fixtures, the latest equipment, the bustle of busy researchers, she is far now from that protected environment, from the regulated necessity of protocol.

In her hotel room, she devotes herself to reading data, she spends more and more time in the code of the sequence, with the horizontal lines that translate incomprehensible metabolic paths. Usually, it's the computer that runs the sequences, reading and recognizing data is an activity reserved for its systems. Sadie reclaims this task, and the act of reading pulls her toward a point of escape, for a little while at least, until her neck interrupts her, a collar of pain.

From the lost horizon of the microscope, the virus survives and continues to multiply in the margins of her gaze, it adapts to the decor of the room, little amphorae on the textured wallpaper, on the black tiles of the shower, in the large glass rectangle of city framed before her. Static crackling in her vision. She knows this hallucination, has never found it shocking. The virus is not just the little box confined to its safe zone. She knows its ubiquity.

These visions, while furtive, take up more and more of her time, prevent her from blotting out the infinite details that make up the reality of her environment. And yet, her ability to think clearly depends on that process of forgetting. Sadie knows that the brain predicts the world more than it perceives it. It's a question of economy, of budgeting available energy. Neurons consume an alarming amount of energy and are therefore expensive to maintain, so the body makes sure it uses them efficiently. Austerity measures are applied to the way we analyze and synthesize our perceptions of reality, continuously simplifying the assimilation of the present for future use. Our present reality exerts an absolutely unreasonable pressure on our system of perception. In order to live at the rhythm of human time, that is, at the rhythm that the organism can sustain with the energy resources available, we must therefore forget about most of our present reality. Sadie knows all this. It does her good to think about it. To feel the intelligence that never fails her, that never lets her down.

When she directs the conscious beam of her attention toward the microscope, she isolates the virus from the rest of the world, her concentration defines the contours of the viral realm. Taken up by the microscope like that, the virus insinuates itself into her reality. The amphorae sizzle on the surfaces, they alter reality. Here, there, the virus touches everything.

Above her, the thick, granular plaster ceiling spreads out to the corners of the wallpapered walls, like paste frozen mid-drip. She imagines the scratches the rough surface would leave if she rubbed against it. There's a knock at the door. She stiffens, holds her breath. She tries to recall whether she'd ordered something, no, the "Do Not Disturb" sign is on the door, whoever it is will leave again. Then she hears Claire's voice through the door. Sadie gets up painfully from the bed where she's been stretched out, gravity drains the fluids from her face, her blood flows back down to her legs. She goes to the door and opens it to find Claire, with Trix behind her. "Sorry to just show up like this, but I hadn't heard from you and I was starting to worry."

Claire tilts her head toward Sadie, a solicitous angle Sadie is getting to know well. Claire speaks and it's like a dance. The two girls come into the room, Trix takes out a set of small speakers, Claire settles into a chair after gently moving a pile of papers, as if to not disturb them, and takes out an electronic joint. Sadie catches Claire's eyes lingering on the characters filling the paper, but Claire is tactful enough to hide her surprise at this strange method. What would be the point of reading, and especially copying out, series of proteins when the computer found no correspondence in the databases? For Claire, who missed most, if not all, of the era of paper, the simple idea of actually reading the virus is bizarre. *Horses* by Patti Smith starts pouring into the room. "This will help you relax," Claire says calmly, handing her the gadget. "You don't look so hot."

Trix scans the room, taking it all in, pretending not to notice the papers spread out over the bed and in small piles on the carpet. "Fancy...," she says, in a complex tone, her sarcasm doesn't completely hide a childish pleasure at opulence. Sadie wants to protest, but she doesn't know how to show them that this is not her world. She wants to express her contempt for the sordid luxury, but she can't figure out how to distance herself from it. She tries to formulate something, but it comes out as mumbling from an imprecise pout. Trix looks at her for a moment, then changes the subject. "So...what are you mad scientists up to these days?"

Claire can't contain her excitement, she starts gushing about their important discoveries, throwing oblique glances at Sadie without interrupting her own flow, as if inviting her to jump into the conversation. She talks about the new Pandoravirus, she talks about Sadie's research, she talks about their incomprehensible finding, she starts listing their latest hypotheses. Her enthusiasm weighs on Sadie. In this new context, she realizes just how familiar Claire has become with the subtleties of the problem. She's creating links, elegant shortcuts that rattle Sadie, who feels like she's short-circuiting. The drugs have overtaken her violently, everything is racing. Claire's words rush into her, but she can only hold onto one idea at a time, if she tries to turn back to a few moments earlier, she stumbles into a blank. Each idea Claire utters hits Sadie with a deluge of meaning that detaches itself from the stream of her speech.

She smoked too much, her skull is tingling. Patti's hallucinatory voice is dancing on shuffle. "Free Money" reminds her of Molly, she tries to summon up a Sunday afternoon, coming down from a night at Scum, Molly making coffee in Sadie's kitchen, wearing a T-shirt that shows off the perfect shape of her breasts, her long, muscled legs lazily sauntering around. Claire's voice pierces the image, comes to her in fragments that flash before her but remain out of reach. She concentrates, takes a deep breath. She knows this moment, its unbearable intensity. She just has to get through it. She's already on the roller coaster, whether she likes it or not, she just has to let go of the handrail.

Patti sings about a jet plane, taking you higher, through the big window, the lights trace patterns in the dark outside, on which the lines of the room are superimposed, then she'll take you down deep, their three silhouettes float between the buildings, beyond the avenues and their minuscule cars... Sadie's liquid thoughts flow in time with the cavalcade of Patti's dream, until the decrescendo of "Break It Up" encourages her to settle into just the right amount of tension. The thoughts that have been swirling endlessly in her head for days, now, through Claire's gestures, suddenly start to breathe. In Claire's hands, in her eyes, her mouth, the twisted, congested outline of ideas is untangled little by little, finds a new mobility in its multiple folds. Sadie still can't grasp the whole thing all at once in her head, but themes appear one after another and produce variations. Claire gives a musicality to her thoughts. An idea comes to Sadie and she lets it in. She lets it generate concepts, unfurl and unroll them in a sequence that Claire catches and threads into a response that surprises Sadie, who takes the time to contemplate the unexpected figure, she lets her imagination feel it out, lets it make its way inside her. The high allows her that flexibility, but it's something else, too, that the high only facilitates: the permeability of thoughts.

Sitting cross-legged on the edge of the bed, Trix listens intently as she taps out the beat. Claire leans toward Trix, toward that attention, twirling her thoughts around with a rebellious confidence, and Sadie now gives over to her delight in the performance. She is rediscovering the pleasure of creating an infinite arrangement of figures at a thousand miles an hour, of dancing theoretically with Claire for Trix, who is following along with their thoughts. It brings her back to the energy of her early days with Régnier, when she discovered that choreography of the intellect. The past triggers something, a spasm spreads through her in small, unpleasant contractions. This young woman's energy affects her, confronts her too directly. With Régnier, the feeling of exaltation is easy, it draws her out of herself. Claire's exuberance requires something else of her.

Here and there, Trix interrupts them, challenges them to develop a concept, to clarify a logical connection. The first few times, the flow of ideas suffers from having to break and shift registers. Sadie is wary, she knows how the thought exercise can derail them, lead them into speculative loops that will never close back up. But then, they find a rhythm. Trix gains confidence and breaks down each notion that is formed into an inner complexity, inviting them deeper into it. Their speech bifurcates, thought moves from one language to another. When they break open the unity of a word, it releases something unpredictable that branches out into several other words. As the tree-like structure grows, they leave more and more bits and pieces behind, conceptual debris multiplying and resurfacing in a disorderly fashion.

Trix asks: "So if you can 'wake up' those viruses from a thousand-year slumber, and just turn them back on and get them to reproduce again, then it's a whole other logic of reproduction and 'descent,' right?" She switches to her halting French: "Can Darwin explain this? I mean, isn't that a whole different logic of time?"

"Yes, exactly, that's what you were saying, Sadie," Claire responds. "The viral particle, the little box of the virus, it can stay in stasis, inert, without producing descendants."

"It doesn't have the same evolutionary pressure, that much is clear," Sadie says. "The viral particle doesn't have a continuous life cycle like a living being."

"That's it! A discontinuous life cycle, that's crazy, we never think like this!" Claire's face lights up at the abundance of ideas.

Until now, Sadie had been trying to close the loops, to shut the countless theoretical drawers. But between Claire's indefatigable curiosity and Trix's conceptual flexibility, she feels the urge to let herself be swept up in the confusion of ideas. They get into it, heads spinning at full speed, Sadie forgets the panic that had been gripping her belly, she forgets to be afraid that the loop won't close.

She's getting close to that vertiginous delight where speech is released from meaning, she feels like she could almost taste Claire's words. The figures make their way into her head, into her nerves, like new creatures to be rediscovered, and Sadie manages to not hold them back, she lets them reproduce their irregular formations and resists the temptation to close her mind to try to capture them, hold them still to better contemplate them, she lets the temptation to name them dissipate in its own energy. While usually each word belongs too much to the world, while she can no longer approach the unknown of her worn-out language, encrusted in the map of knowledge, Claire's voice recreates the virus. Sadie knows the moment will end soon, she is barely aware of it before it is slipping away from her.

X

After a while—an hour, twenty minutes, who knows in that elastic time—the excitement wanes. Sadie loses the continuity of thought again, her brain fogs. She begins a proposition she can't finish and lets it unravel, hanging in the air before her. The high is over. Sadie hits the vaporizer again, but the air only gets heavier and heavier, her thoughts stiffening. Claire is still throwing sentences at her, asking her questions, but Sadie's head is full of cotton. Her brain is an inert mass regaining its measure in the world.

The next morning, when she wakes up, she sees that Molly has emailed her a playlist. Sadie can sense an obligation, in the tone and in the format. She downloads it, it starts strong. The first measures of a distorted drumming that Sadie recognizes, she knows it well, then the bass, passed through effects, filters, reverb. One of the first songs Molly shared with her in the early days of their friendship, a contemporary cover of a pop hit from the sixties.

The playlist moves on to "Land," from Patti Smith's *Horses*. The track brings back a forgotten fragment of the day before, along with the atmosphere and the thoughts that formed within it. It pulls up a strand of time. The last time she saw Molly, the morning she left for Montreal, Sadie stood on the landing, listening to Molly's footsteps, faster and faster, lighter and lighter, as she headed down to the street.

One by one, songs she knows, songs Molly has sent her before. She is telling her something with this chain of their shared moments strung together. In the background of this necklace of songs, Sadie can hear a declaration that they have come full circle, in a painfully elegant way. Molly leaves her with nothing left to discover. By going back over these tracks, Molly is creating a vanitas for her, the *memento mori* of their story. Sadie puts the playlist on repeat. She doesn't respond to Molly.

Usually, she immerses herself in headphones to keep out the world around her, but she usually also has her eyes attached to a microscope. All her senses plugged in. Usually, she wanders down Molly's desirous paths and encounters in new sounds the familiar images of her body language. But this succession of overly familiar songs, covers saturated with a shared history, clutters the listening experience with many Mollys. Sadie always knew Molly would take off someday. She always knew she was capable of this small act of cruelty. Always knew that one day Molly would disappear herself, leaving Sadie with the many skins she'd shed.

Sadie plays through the tracks like the mala beads that count off a precious mantra. She wallpapers her imagination, plasters her interior with Molly's many skins, many poses.

Her headphones on, she returns to her metabolic lists. What's the point of answering, really, she won't waste her breath, instead she'll pour it into the tracks that make Molly still exist, Molly of a thousand hands, Molly of the hardest heart, Sadie plays Molly in all her different arrangements: Anika – Patti – Julz – Vivien – Dolores – David – Myrna – Nancy – Françoise – Gina – Morrissey – Will – Masumi – Marianne – Yōsui – Nina – Serge – Selda...

When she gets to the end, she starts again from the top, bead by bead.

Inside this room, she has everything she needs, and more. She orders bland meals at outrageous prices, all she has to do is press the button with the image of a bell on the bedside table telephone, and someone will bring her more lukewarm eggs that taste like water, slightly stale bagels, and coffee, lots of coffee, all day long, which wrecks her guts. One of these days they'll kick her to the curb, when she maxes out the lab's credit card. Sadie, who had always turned away from such ostentation, disgusted by the unoriginal puerility of the wealthy, now sinks into the sticky luxury of the room.

She had always lived frugally. The principle of efficiency exerted a constant, reassuring pressure on her. She makes do with very little and produces a lot, what she calls her margin of freedom. Maybe that's why her life is so perfectly suited to the scientific method. To the imperative of the most cautious hypothesis. Knowledge is not a luxury. Think economically, see only truth. The most cautious, parsimonious hypothesis... What if she came back to Marseille with something else? What if she came back with a luxurious hypothesis, or, worse, a luxurious idea?

The economy of her daily life is reversed here. In this room where everything is provided for her—filtered air, bottled water, clean towels left outside her door with rolls of toilet paper and notepads—she doesn't worry about the cost. The bell will toll eventually, but in the meantime, the straitjacket of her days is loosening. The ratio shifts, and as the pressure of her daily routine is relaxed, her mind allows itself a few superfluous operations.

When she disconnects from the sound of Molly, she spends a long time stretched out on the bed, listening to the backwash of liquids travelling through the hotel's plumbing, the rumbling of the ventilation system, the rolling of suitcases through the corridor, the rare voices that reach her in a muffled murmur. The building whirrs with these currents that move through it and resonate inside her. It is answered by the incessant noise of her different bodily functions that until now were silent, undifferentiated. The rumbling of her digestion, the wheeze of her breath, and then the more gelatinous sounds, her swallowing, and, in moments, a kind of viscous sucking that she eventually identifies as her eyes moving in their mucous membrane. Reality is louder these days. It's as if she is losing the ability to forget. She orders copious meals and leaves most of the food untouched. She eats only the soft-boiled egg, which she can hear trickling down her esophagus and deep into her stomach.

Her father tries to call her, but she can't bring herself to answer, she doesn't want his voice in her ear. She doesn't forget. In her mother, the sedimentary soil of memory is rising to the surface as if bubbling up from the depths of the past. And Sadie is still struggling to resolve in her mind how that woman who remains, somewhere inside her, the sum of all her experiences, her losses, her suffering, her struggles, and her renunciations, how that woman was able to see again a world in which she was waiting, longing for touch. Dementia has allowed her mother to relearn this, it has reminded her that she had already known, in some ancient, previous life, how to need.

Her mother's expertise, however, had always been that of a mastery of surfaces. She never learned to open up flesh, unlike her husband, she didn't operate, she expanded her practice to diagnostic interpretation. Sadie's father had perfected the art of closing skulls back up after having altered their vital circuits. Along the way, he acquired a bad reputation among his colleagues for monopolizing the operating room by spending too much time on his sutures. His patients were endlessly grateful to him for the time he took—which was absolutely unreasonable in the eyes of the colleagues he kept waiting—dedicated to repairing his invasion into their head. Perhaps the art of repair had prepared him, in the end, for taking care of her. Perhaps it was even him that, through his lavish care, went and fished out, from the disorder of the times in which her mother was now living, that very old fragment of life. Through an abundance of care—is that not what he was once reproached for, an unreasonable generosity that exceeded the time allotted?—perhaps he had responded to a need that his wife had long ago forgotten existed, awakening a primitive state in her. He had finally managed to unearth, from deep inside her, the ability to accept help. He made her his final patient, for her he tracked no hours, devoted an almost certainly unreasonable amount of time, but together they no longer skimp on delirium.

Sadie continues to cohabitate with the virus even if she doesn't go visit it at the hospital anymore, she goes over the translations of the code into proteins again and again. The sequences of letters determine the specific order of assembly of each amino acid that makes up the protein. She compares them with the proteins listed in other members of the family. Sometimes she has déjà vu and looks for the protein in the lists of relatives. Most of the time, that feeling ends up evaporating in the course of inconclusive searches. She lives inside that translation, in the language that can teach her the ultimate aim of the virus, the way it inhabits the world.

MATASSLVFSGSLAALPLPNELLAAVLSFLDPVDS
VAASRVQRLWRAFAPPLCAFGPAYTAQLAARGHLD
VLQWARADGCPCDTVAASAAARAGHLHVLQ
WLYDNKCPWNGDACDEAAKGGHLEVLQWL
RANGCPWDPWLCCVRAAEHGHLDVLQWLHANG
CPLSESVCIGAAEHGHLDVLQWLCANGCPWD
KRVAVRAAAGGHLDVLQWLHANGCAPNADAC
FAAAMRGHLQVIQWLRANNWPWDHNVCF
RAVVNGHLEVLQWLHANGCPWYDGASVCAARC
GQWAVLKWFCANGFPWDADDVDNADDVDN

ADACAKAAQEGRLDMLQWLHARGRYSWDTD
VCAEAAAGGHLDVLQWLCANGCPWDAHA
CAEAAREGHLEVLQWLRANGCPWDERACKR
AVREGHLETMQWLWANGCPRNTDACTRAALK
SAVDTVRWIRREAGGADEHMRAFADMRNRLAVLR
WLRANGCPWHRWTCANAGLSHYADTLCRAVERIP

When she tires of comparing, of moving from one database to another, when her eyes start to lose focus in the brightness of the computer screen, she starts transcribing. Headphones on, Molly's playlist on repeat, she takes the hotel letterhead and recopies the series of letters. When she fills one page, she rotates it and writes over the now vertical lines, and then does the same thing on the back. She saw the method used years ago in the library at Trinity College in Dublin. She'd escaped from a conference for a few hours and gone for a walk in the university gardens, among the trees with winding, sinuous branches hardy enough to survive the winter. In the narrow library, which looked like an ancient temple, where walls of books rose to a high vaulted ceiling of dark wood, she found, displayed under glass, letters from the nineteenth century in that strange criss-cross writing, a three-dimensional script from a time when paper was rare and precious, even for the aristocracy. How did those cor-respondents manage to decode messages written in such cunningly parsimonious script? Perhaps their eyes were accustomed to putting order back into the layers of writing. For Sadie, paper is not a big expense. Dozens and dozens of sheets accumulate on the desk, the dresser, and soon the floor, covered in series of capital letters.

She copies until her eyes are exhausted, her jaw clenched shut. The more she transcribes, the less she can see, at times her writing drifts out of its straight lines. In the blur, she continues to string letters together and, by force of their repetition and recurrence, the order of the alphabet starts to lose its predominance. She fills sheet after sheet, she assembles the particles orphaned of meaning until she gets completely confused, loses the thread. Then her vision narrows, and when she manages to focus again, she can't find the place where she left off, the point that is different from the rest.

The act of writing out the virus brings her body back to an era when she still worked with paper all the time, when researchers printed out the analyses to compare letters by hand. Her own body had integrated the exponential development of bioinformatics. She would have phases like this when they were hard at work on a new specimen in the lab. Periods of time when she lived inside the writing and rewriting of the virus. Bent over her pages, she thinks of Dostoevsky's Prince Myshkin, whose knowledge of ancient calligraphy prompts the Epanchins to take him in. She, too, is a scribe, and must try, through an absolutely mind-numbing activity, to render the clean and remarkable character of this writing.

Yet, the translations she copies and recopies are not the virus's original language. They are an intermediary space. This has always been her task, as a translator of the parasitic world, in the gap between what she observes and the human structures that try to name it. Her loyalty should, by force of circumstance, lie with human language, but as she goes through the letters, she feels herself belonging to the act of transport, she becomes the relationship, halfway between the formation of the virus and its representation in our language.

But the language we use to try to name it speaks less of the life of the virus than of the way it spreads through the world. The sequences of letters name only a present that is always already past. When she observes it, when she witnesses the visible stages of the infection, the intelligence of the virus is already elsewhere, someplace we can't yet see it. We are always a step behind in the parasitic life cycle, we can only translate the virus in terms of its aim, while it is busy renewing itself, continuously transforming. And with the virus posing her the question of how it functions, its ultimate purpose still illegible, she has nothing to hold onto. Like in Chinese grammar, where only verbs are considered alive, as opposed to nouns, which are seen as dead words, what she manages to name of the virus is inert, its life is elsewhere. Her hand, exhausted from all the rewriting, can no longer complete the letters, it allows itself inelegant freedoms, her writing is destabilized, her Cs look like Gs, her script starts to blur.

Molly's beats change from one track to the next, setting a tempo for Sadie, who does not pause in her work. The monads of music return, each track refracting a whole world, as the snippets of code return, as the virus reproduces itself elsewhere, everywhere, in a language she knows nothing about.

The virus has survived in the world through its mastery of the code, and Sadie works from that parasitic knowledge to translate the traces of its survival. Her work as a translator of the viral world has been directed, all these years, toward the ultimate goal: to have the virus recognized among the order of the living. But what does it mean for a virus to be alive? She doesn't understand, she feels further and further from understanding. Yet it shouldn't surprise her, from the beginning she has worked to dismantle the strict limits of our notion of the virus. She has always recognized the inadequacy of her tools, an intellectual position that subjects her to the tension of a partly impossible task. But now, the inadequacy of her grammar is something she feels intimately. The life of the virus is too big an idea, too costly, and it is threatening to subluxate her brain.

Alone, drifting down the corridor of translation, with no language to touch the virus, she could turn back, return to the shores of the human world, yes, she should rejoin that other existence where she no longer really knows how to play the game.

Paper piles up, accumulating in the room, she's stopped letting the housekeepers in. Even when irrepressible urges drive her to the bathroom, she takes her computer or pad of paper with her, and as she empties herself of liquid waste, she continues to generate shapes. The mass of paper is far larger than what her mind can hold, they are scribbled over on every side and scattered all over the floor, she has stopped trying to connect them to a thread.

> *You should follow the thread, though, Sadie.*
> *All genes have a story.*

Régnier, she can't detach herself from him, she can't give him up. Régnier, this can't be reduced to him, it exceeds the box of the individual, she is Régnier too, that's what happens when the subject escapes the envelope of the individual, the creative impulse, when it transcends the particle and continues through it. Régnier, she can't remove herself from the equation with a single stroke. Because that too, by an impulse that begins with her, transcends

itself and enters the system, learns its code, and gives it an extension, carries out the translation.

We cannot create something larger from something smaller.

If only it were a question of denying the proposition, if only it
were a question of disavowal. She could start her life over. But he
has taught her what negation does. It was all there, from the
beginning, the first seminar, he taught her that negation, when
repeated, becomes a rhythm, a scansion by which another reality
is created.

We cannot create something from nothing.

It's not a question of denying with a contradicting statement. It's
not a question of just walking away. She has given a syntax to
their intelligence, their shared madness, to work that was asking
to be translated into the world.

Pandora is her work too. With their combined intelligence, they
have stretched a grid over the reality of the virus, together they
have developed the language to name it, speak it.

Some energy pushes her beyond her strength, even as she is
squinting to the point of blindness, she keeps going, straining her
eyes, deforming her hand, destroying her brain, running the inad-
equate language through her neurons, stretched thin in an
ongoing attempt... This is the point at which she could almost
touch their intelligence, but in the attempt, she can't manage to
release the tension, her clenched jaw is locked in with the muscles

of her throat, her shoulders, as if all the musculature of her neck was welded into an armour attaching her head to her torso, her movements are limited, she can see the amphorae developing on the margins of the tree of life, but she can't turn her head, she would like to twist herself far enough, she is ready to break, if necessary, to give in for good, to join the intelligence of the losers, the ones who waste their time, the energy of evolution's losers, she would like to rid herself of her ancestry, she imagines herself going back along the branches, coming back as sap flowing against the current of time, against the vehicles of evolution up to the last common ancestor, before the invention of cellular life, getting rid of the code of cohesion, she imagines it for a moment, that's what she wants, the knowledge of dispersion, and she tries hard, since the fortress of effort continues to hold her, preventing her from getting rid of herself. Her intelligence will not let her fall.

She isn't sleeping anymore. It started one night when the questions woke her up and she couldn't get back to sleep. Normally, she would have just read, but she couldn't focus on the words, there was too much to do, too much to think about. The next morning, instead of feeling the effects of the insomnia, she was overflowing with energy. The next night, instead of catching up on the sleep she'd lost the night before, she slept even less, and at the break of day found herself with even more energy. This cycle continues but she no longer sees a clear distinction between day and night, they no longer belong to different regimes. Since night no longer gives the day any finality, other sequences begin to mean more than the law of the solar system. The coffee she ingests at all hours makes her shaky, liquefying her insides by tuning her digestion to the cadence of her heart, arrhythmic and frantic.

Chewing is exhausting, the rumination of her jaw now gives her the impression she is continually masticating the same fibre, squeaking horribly between her teeth, against the mucosal lining of her mouth, each swallow sounds its deafening stirrings, sending vibrations through her digestive system down to the bottom of her abdomen. She orders raw eggs and mixes in a little sugar for taste, producing a mucus that slides easily down her throat, caressing her esophagus. She absorbs without chewing the miscellany of the world.

Ding! A notification. Ding! Claire is sending her another message, since she hasn't responded to the previous ones.

to: asst.director@virolab-marseille.fr
from: claire.jean-baptiste@mcgill.qc.ca
subject: de novo?

Sadie,

I'm at the McGill library. Funny how I immediately want to write in English when I come back here. I tried calling you at the hotel, but they couldn't reach you.

After our conversation with Trix the other night, I wrote to a few colleagues in bioinformatics, and I talked to this girl I slightly know who does transcriptomics, and also this guy who knows a lot about proteomics, and we started chatting about intergenic regions. The girl was telling me about Mar Albà in Barcelona and her work on the appearance of new genes. Anyway, I started looking through articles on *de novo* genes and I found one from 2012 about yeast and the creation of *de novo* genes. I pulled up a couple others too, I'll send them to you.

Sadie, I think we've got something here. It's been right in front of us the whole time. You always say we can't create genes from nothing, every gene has a story. But what if that's just it?

What if this virus created its own genes, *de novo?*

Ding! The answer is at the door. The long awaited eureka! An intestinal spasm at each signal. She hears Claire's call, she sees the words "*de novo*," she recognizes the name of Mar Albà, but the signal of what has been set in motion doesn't stop, that click keeps clicking, click clicking, unclicking, reclicking, decomposing and recomposing. No matter how hard she tries to focus her whole mind on grasping the meaning of these words—*de novo*—she can't do it.

De novo. The virus, creator of its own genes. But what does that say about a thing that transcends its own box, a life that transcends the envelope of the individual, a relationship? That the virus reinvents its own code. What does it mean, though, when the virus spills over the limits of what it means to be itself? This new thing cannot be contained.

Claire sends her question across the city, holds out a net for her to drop into. All she needs is to let herself fall into it, rest a little, see how that feels. Sadie doesn't answer, she doesn't stop the question as it's forming, she recognizes in Claire the need one might have, the need for another mind, a mind intimately acquainted with the question that can give the still nebulous impulse the shape of the idea.

What would happen if nobody stopped the movement of thought? She knows how much you need someone, in the worldless space of speculation, to give credence to an idea. She thinks about Claire's need for someone to be a vessel for the impulse.

In the words—*de novo*—two wide eyes are staring up at her, that detach—*ovo*—the egg it contains, its albumen not coagulating. Between what flows and the idea, everything is possible.

This thing addresses her, wants to come in, asks to be thought, but Sadie doesn't know how to make herself a vessel. Because in that question she hears too much of Claire's need, speaking to her, running through the city, taking a route Sadie can't really predict, that need doesn't respect the grid of avenues, it knows nothing of direction, it knows only how to pulse, and in Sadie a pulsation responds, what was earlier a spasm now stretches, becomes a beat, what was a contraction in her, a tightening, now loosens, moves from her intestines up to her solar plexus, and through her heart to meet her throat, her head.

The need is disgusting, it speaks to her in the language of entrails, of mixed matter, of decomposition. A slime travels up the ducts, an acid taste softens her mouth. Her neck still tries to form a barrier, to establish a separation, refusing to yield.

Her head, overheated and pounding, is drawn to the coolness of the big window, she leans against the glass but it's warm from the direct sun. The currents are flowing again, liberated by the melting ice, awakening prehistoric debris. *De novo,* the virus invents its own language, she does not yet have the words to respond to the question. She suddenly feels very naked, without the safety net of language, without the stranglehold of skill.

It was the nudity, that night. It was the nudity that forced Sadie to take her mother in her arms, to hold her body close, to carry her as if she were a part of herself. If she had been clothed, Sadie thinks in a burst of lucidity, she might have taken her by the arm, at most supported her weight a little, and guided her toward the house, maybe up the steps, and left her there at the doorstep. It was the nudity, that night, that forced her to take responsibility for her, as if part of herself, to take care of her as if she were a cancer whose mass had begun to grow, to occupy a growing place in her, to deform her with its need, to shape her with its whites.

Her eyes widen, letting in the light through the window, letting in the swell of the avenues, the boulevards, the buzz of the city she can hear clearly through the thick glass. She recognizes the rumbling of the city that carried her, a very long time ago, the city in which she was carried, the white, white light of America, the sand of the glass that separates her from the city disintegrates, reality becomes an undercooked dough and,

with a great cry!

Sadie becomes part of the raw moment, an impulse overloads the nucleus of each cell, the cry moves through the tissue of the sacred nerves that connect her pelvis to her head, and it comes undone, in that cry that gives way, she calls for help, she calls Claire, and then it spills over the name, it comes out of her mouth, but from a place further off than her intelligence, it floods her head and continues in tremolo, calls up another memory and then another, the cry disperses among the multitude it was holding, it calls up Orphée and his boat, a raft for her pain, they float down the artery below, flowing so fast it looks like rapids, a liquid convoy, it calls up Veronica, who will bring a little lawlessness to the city centre, shakes loose another memory, yet another, a memory of rats, so many rats, of precarious associations to spread through the world, to spill over history, how to name that which speaks of a life still strange to us, that life can only howl so that's what it does, it is a wail from before the partition of the individual, it is a cry that is distorted in its need of others, its need of everyone, do you hear it (you who are listening to this boundless need), do you hear it resounding and multiplying, a need nothing can contain, there is no syntax for it, there is nothing left but to sink into it.

TRANSLATOR'S NOTE

Fragments from Sigmund Freud's *A General Introduction to Psycho-analysis* on page 11 appear here in G. Stanley Hall's translation.

Lines from Hesiod's *Works and Days* on pages 23 and 24 are quoted in Hugh G. Evelyn-White's translation.

ACKNOWLEDGEMENTS

The translator would like to thank Katia Grubisic for her inspired edits, and Clara Dupuis-Morency for her collaboration and counsel on this translation. Many thanks as well to Jo Ramsay for copy-editing, and to Jay and Hazel Millar and everyone at Book*hug for their thoughtful work on this book.

PHOTO: LES MAROIS

ABOUT THE AUTHOR

Clara Dupuis-Morency was born in Quebec City and lives in Montreal. Her first novel, *Mère d'invention*, was a finalist for the Prix des libraires du Québec, the Prix du CALQ for Work by an Emerging Artist, and the France-Quebec prize, Les Rendez-vous du premier roman. She also works as a translator and is the mother of twin girls.

PHOTO: RICHARD LAM

ABOUT THE TRANSLATOR

Newfoundland-native Aimee Wall is a writer and translator. Her translations include Vickie Gendreau's novels *Testament* (2016) and *Drama Queens* (2019), and Jean-Philippe Baril Guérard's *Sports and Pastimes* (2017). Her acclaimed debut novel, *We, Jane*, was nominated for nine literary prizes including the Amazon Canada First Novel Award, the BMO Winterset Award, the ReLit Award for Fiction, and the Scotiabank Giller Prize longlist. Wall lives in Montreal.

COLOPHON

Manufactured as the first English edition of
Sadie X
In the fall of 2023 by Book*hug Press

Edited for the press by Katia Grubisic
Copy-edited by Jo Ramsay
Proofread by Laurie Siblock

Printed in Canada

bookhugpress.ca